Anthony Masters is a hugely experienced and well-known author. As well as writing thrillers and biographies for adults, he has written many titles for young people, including *Streetwise*, which was nominated for the Carnegie Medal. He also runs Book Explosions – workshops that open up works of children's literature, using a combination of adventure training, dance, drama, simulation and writing.

He has been the subject of a BBC2 film, *Inside Story*, and is also a regular broadcaster. Married, with three children, he lives in Sussex.

TWISTER

ANTHONY MASTERS

MACMILLAN
CHILDREN'S BOOKS

The poem on page 144 was used on student posters in Palermo during the march against the Mafia in 1963 and was attributed to Brecht. It appears in *On Persephone's Island* by Mary Taylor Simeti (Penguin Travel Library 1988) and is used with the kind permission of Penguin Books Limited.

First published 1995 by Macmillan Children's Books

a division of Macmillan Publishers Limited
25 Eccleston Place London SW1W 9NF
and Basingstoke

Associated companies throughout the world

ISBN 0 330 336843

3 5 7 9 8 6 4 2

A CIP catalogue record for this book is available from the British Library

Phototypeset by Intype, London
Printed and bound in Great Britain by
Mackays of Chatham PLC, Chatham, Kent

PROLOGUE

TIM STOOD outside the boat-yard office, listening to his stepfather, Will, talking on the phone in Sicilian. The reason Tim had finally decided to spy on him was because Will regularly made the private calls at about 10 p.m. and often returned home to the pub where they lived, looking drawn and tense. When Mum had commented on his appearance, Will had quickly said he was settling some business and, when pressed, he added that the business had to do with selling his bar in Fortuna. Mum accepted the story but Tim was curious. Was his stepfather a con-man, swindling his mother out of all her money, or was he Mr Nice Guy after all? Tim desperately hoped Will was the latter, but could never be sure. He liked his stepfather all right and wanted to like him more, but the only way to achieve that was to find out about him. For Will was a stranger, a man who had come into Tim's life only a few months ago.

Tim had been spying on Will for almost a week now, his curiosity rising. Obviously his stepfather was under some kind of pressure – pressure that Mum put down to 'business problems' – but Tim reckoned there might be something else. Did he have another life? Another family? Another side to him that Tim and his mother didn't know? Was he straight? Was he a crook? Who *was* he?

Tim hugged the side of the old railway carriage that served as the boat-yard's office and inched his way along. Then he saw Dino, Will's son, walk in from the path by the creek, looking angry, glancing neither to the right nor to the left, obviously intent on seeking out his father. He heard the click of the replaced telephone receiver and the sound of raised voices, beginning in Sicilian and then abruptly breaking into English. At first Tim couldn't hear what they were saying, but slowly, listening intently, he began to understand the argument.

'Your English is lousy,' Will was saying. 'You have to practise.'

'I don't trust you. Who you speak?'

'Who were you speaking to – that's the correct phrase.' Will sounded pompous as he always did when he was correcting someone.

'Who were you speaking to?' said Dino sulkily, resenting being reprimanded as always.

'Luigi. He phoned me.'

'To say the Don is angry?'

'Something like that.' Will was too casual.

'What you expect?' Suddenly the relationship

had altered, with Dino as the critic rather than Will.

'No more. I was a fool.' He sounded slightly chastened.

'I don't trust you.'

'No?' Will laughed irritably.

'You swear it was Luigi?'

'Who else could it have been?'

Dino was silent. Tim guessed he didn't want to provoke his father.

'Come *on*. Who else?' Will demanded, and Tim was shocked to hear the unfamiliar menace in his stepfather's voice. He had always been so understanding, had such tolerance. 'You tell me.' The menace had intensified, hard and ugly.

'You not hit me.' Dino suddenly sounded terrified.

'Then tell me.'

'I say – nothing.'

'You wanted to get away as much as I did. You wanted to make a new beginning too.'

'The Don won't let you. We should never have come to England.'

'He's got to. Now shut your mouth. We'd better go back home or they'll start thinking that—'

Tim fled. At all costs he mustn't be seen. As he ran back to the pub, he wondered yet again who his stepfather really was. And what might he and his mother – what would they – start thinking?

CHAPTER ONE

TIM FIRST saw them on his way home from school, not knowing whether to be scared or curious. In fact he was both. Not many strangers parked in such a remote part of the countryside. Tim cycled past the Renault as fast as he could, squinting into the car as he went. The driver was elderly and wore a formal suit. He had a small moustache and white hair, but his companion was younger, with a casual checked shirt, a long, narrow face, his hair glistening black.

They were watching the pub – Tim was sure about that.

The run-down, closed-up pub and boat-yard near All-Hallows Creek in the Kent marshes were collectively called Whispers. The old inn sign depicted two men whispering to the landlord behind the bar. Tim could only just make out the figures because the paint was cracking badly after decades of exposure to the winds from the estuary. Mum said they were smugglers and she was glad that at least the name hadn't been corny – like The Smugglers. She thought Whispers was romantic and had almost bought the place for its haunting name. Certainly there wasn't much else to recommend it, for all the buildings had been abandoned a long time ago.

The Swale estuary was a few hundred metres away and there was a wide track leading down from the pub. That was where the two strangers sat in their car. They had binoculars and appeared to be occasionally surveying the nature reserve, but if they were bird-watchers, they were very passive ones, to say the least.

Will, of course, had the answer. Tim sometimes thought his new stepfather had the answer to everything. Not only had he persuaded Mum to give up working at the bakery and buy the defunct pub and boat-yard, but he had also convinced her that he was going to turn both into big commercial successes. The pub had closed five years ago for lack of trade and the flat above it was cold and damp. The boat-yard had staggered on for a couple of seasons more but had then gone bankrupt.

'They're photographers,' Will claimed. 'I had a word with them. Don't like strangers hanging around – not unless I know what they're up to. but those two knocked to say what they were doing. Apparently they've been commissioned by a magazine to get some shots of the reserve.'

Will had come into Tim and his mother's lives a few months ago – six years after his dad had pushed off to live with another woman. Tim had seen his father occasionally for a while, but the visits soon petered out and he never saw him again. The hurt was still there, but he had more or less forgotten his face now. That helped.

He and Mum had stayed on in Torridge, the light industrial town where Tim had been born and now went to school. Although he was tall for his age, he was unassertive, despised by many of the boys for his lack of machismo, and while his shoulder-length blond hair and clear skin made him attractive to girls, he usually felt awkward with them. Tim was shy and didn't have that many friends. He had a passionate interest in long-distance running, and when he wasn't doing that he would read. Then Aunty Betty had left Mum all her money and almost at the same time Will had turned up. With Dino.

Will was British, but he had lived and worked in Sicily for years until his marriage had folded. This had led him to return to England with his sixteen-year-old Sicilian son, Dino, where he took over as manager of a little coffee shop in Torridge – a place where coffee shops were viewed with suspicion. Tea rooms were acceptable, but the Orinoco was regarded as outlandish, with its mock palms, coloured tablecloths and frothing Espresso machine. As a result, trade had been slow.

From the very beginning, Tim had been suspicious of Will, partly because he had so suddenly come into their lives, but largely because he knew his mother had told Will about the money she had inherited. At first his mother's growing relationship with the coffee shop manager had seemed all too well connected with the inheritance, but when Tim knew him better he had tried to banish these fears, mainly because he liked Will and wanted his future stepfather to be straight.

Will was a big, rangy, clean-shaven, charismatic man, fluent in both Sicilian and Italian, but although he *did* seem to have an answer for everything, Will also had a good sense of humour and a genuine warmth that was spontaneous and attractive. Like Tim, he loved books; like Tim, he was a fan of Charles Dickens – and, like Tim, he loved running. They took to jogging together in the early mornings and they had been to Rochester and Chatham and Broadstairs, following the trail of Dickens locations and characters. It had entered Tim's head several times that Will might be doing this just to get in with Tim's mother, but he had pushed away the doubts because he needed the relationship so much.

Dino was a different proposition. Small, dark

and handsome in a rather sullen way, he was a trainee chef and wanted to open his own restaurant. He was at a catering college and at sixteen, as opposed to Tim's fourteen, his only other interest was girls. In Torridge Tim had watched him enviously, seeing him use his Sicilian charm to great effect, but back at Whispers, Dino was sultry, quarrelsome and often on bad terms with the father he seemed to resent, although he had taken the radical step of coming to England with him.

Despite his liking for Will, Tim still regarded him and Dino as strangers. Not complete strangers like the bird-watchers, but strangers nevertheless.

'What do you know about him?' Tim had asked when his mother told him she would like to marry Will. He hadn't been surprised – he had seen it coming – but he knew he had to challenge her. She had made the announcement a few months after Aunty Betty's sudden demise and generous legacy and Tim's doubts were at their height.

'Not a lot.' She had smiled at him affectionately. 'But I've got to take my chances. I'm not saying that I wasn't suspicious of Will's intentions when we first met but, let's face it, Tim – who's going to take an interest in a middle-aged woman like me?'

'A woman with money,' Tim had added.

'I know,' his mother had replied impatiently. 'OK – suppose he does want a bit of security. Does that matter?'

'He might murder you,' Tim had said melo-dramatically, only half believing in what he was saying.

She had grinned. 'Don't worry. I can look after myself, and besides I'm not going to have a joint account with Will – or sign up any insurance policies!' Mum had laughed, as if the idea of him harming her was utterly ridiculous. 'I'm sure he's OK, Tim.'

But he knew that she just *wanted* Will to be OK. Like he did.

'Shouldn't you know more about him?' Tim had been determined to go on being suspicious.

She had sighed. 'All I know is this. Will was born in south London, went to the local school, started out in his dad's second-hard car business, read a book a day, got restless, went to Sicily, met Carla, ran a bar, helped out at a friend's boat-yard, fathered Dino, bust up with Carla – and moved back here. Enough for you?'

'Isn't his story a bit thin?' he had asked, keeping up the pressure.

'So is life.' Marian, Tim's mother, was small, still young-looking, with the same striking blonde hair as her son. She loved to have fun – drinking and dancing till the small hours – but she wasn't stupid and she had a tremendous sense of purpose. Once she seized on something she stuck to it. Or someone. 'Just let yourself like him,' she had continued firmly. 'And I don't want to sit on the money. I want to use it.'

'And lose it?' Tim knew he had sounded like a real spoil-sport. He had wanted her to convince him about his future stepfather.

'On Whispers? Think of the potential.'

'Potential? You sound like Will. It's a dump.'

'Only because it was mismanaged. And it's his first love. Boats. He used to deliver yachts all over the Med.'

'So he says.'

'And there's the pub for Dino to cook in. Might turn into a five-star restaurant one day.'

'Yeah.'

'Come on, Tim! I know what you're thinking. You like Whispers as much as I do. You can't fool me.'

And she was right. Despite its air of dereliction, he had loved moving into the pub, and if he didn't really trust Will, the adventure, the returning sense of family all gave him a tremendous thrill. Torridge had been the ugliest place on earth; even his mother's sense of fun had found little outlet there. Tim had hated to see her depressed – sometimes he thought he was the adult and she the child.

Will, looking flash in a narrow pin-stripe suit, had taken him aside after the registry office wedding. 'You've got to trust me, Tim,' he had said. 'I know it's difficult but I'll see you're all right – and your mum. And let's do a bit of graft on Dino together, all of us, shall we? I know he's not always Mr Sunshine.'

Now they had been at Whispers for three months, surrounded by the wildlife on the muddy creek and the marsh with its stark, flat beauty. Slowly Tim had begun to learn the names of the wild flowers and herbs and become a keen bird-watcher.

Will had been working incredibly hard, getting up at six every day to restore the little eighteenth century pub. Now it was late spring and the days were long; as a result he rarely finished until eight and never took any time off. Slowly but surely the two little bars and the restaurant were coming back to life again.

Will and Mum were obviously happy together and it was a tremendous pleasure to see her confidence returning. Tim knew she was sharing at last, feeling needed, rather than battling away on her own in the bakery. What was more, he had expected to feel jealous of Will, to be excluded, but his stepfather seemed to have a sixth sense about Tim's relationship with his mother and went out of his way to respect it – and to nurture his own slowly building friendship with his stepson.

Even Dino helped, particularly in the refurbishment of the restaurant. Mum worked on the kitchen, and when she wasn't doing that she was trying to make something of the dilapidated flat upstairs. As for Tim, he felt less uptight these days and had even made some friends at school. Things were slowly looking up.

Now, as he cycled along the track that wound past the creek, Tim negotiated the huge pot-holes that had come from disuse, looking ahead curiously, wondering if the Renault would be parked there again. It wasn't.

There were tyre marks, however, and as it had rained earlier that afternoon he was sure they were fresh. They were also deep as if a car, possibly the Renault, had turned and made off quickly.

Then he saw Dino lying in the ditch. He was covered in blood.

CHAPTER TWO

TIM ALMOST fell off his bike but, skidding to a halt, his long legs just managed to act as a brake.

'Dino!'

'Yes?' the Sicilian boy sounded strangely normal.

'Stay there – I'm coming. Try not to move,' Tim gabbled, vaguely remembering a first aid course he had been on years ago.

'It's only paint.'

'*What*?' Then he saw the up-ended tin: WALPA-MUR VERMILION. Someone had poured it over Dino's head, and his bike was also in the ditch, badly buckled and with some of the spokes broken on the back wheel.

Tim climbed down. 'What happened?'

'What you think?' Dino sat up, his accent thickening. His day-to-day English was improving, but crisis always made it worse.

'Who did it?'

'College.'

'College?' Tim didn't understand.

'You stupid?' Dino slowly stood up, glowering at him, the paint dripping on to his stylish fawn jersey and dark trousers.

'Tell me who did it!' persisted Tim.

'Students.'

'Students?'

'Why repeat?' Dino was concealing something in his hand. It was obviously a screwed-up piece of paper.

'What's that you've got?'

'Nothing.'

'In your hand?'

'Nothing!'

Tim suddenly remembered the photographers in the Renault. Dino's bike was only a metre away from the car tracks, and what about the broken spokes?

'You don't mean the photographers?' he asked. 'The two guys in the Renault?'

'I don't,' he replied angrily. 'You find it funny?' He looked belligerent.

'Of course I don't. I was just—'

'Those students. I get girls. They don't. So they punish me.'

'What shall I do?' Tim couldn't think how to help him.

'Take the bike,' he snapped.

*

14

Marian was furious that the students had waylaid Dino, and she talked about writing to the principal of the college. She went on ranting as she gently applied a thick wad of cotton wool saturated with cleansing gel to his face. Slowly most of the paint came off, although it was very difficult to get it out of his thick, black, close-cropped hair.

Tim went out into the boat-yard. Most of the craft were hulks, the jetties had either collapsed or were in considerable disrepair and grass sprouted from the concrete, but it was a time of day he loved; the tide was full, there was no wind and the water was lapping at the grassy sides of the creek.

Will, wearing only an old pair of shorts and trainers, was staring moodily at a derelict wooden yacht. He looked bronzed and fit, but taken off guard Tim could see that his face, screwed up against the sun, had a hunted look and he jumped slightly as Tim approached.

'Hi.'

'Will—'

'I'm going to restore her.' He burst into a flurry of words as if worried that Tim might have detected his mood. 'Used to belong to old Jackson. But when we bought this place, we bought the *Green Lady* as well. I reckon—'

'Will. I've got something to *tell* you.'

'Well?'

'It's Dino. Some kids from his college threw red

15

paint over him.' As Tim began to explain he saw the creeping horror in his stepfather's eyes. It was a surprisingly strong reaction to a student prank.

CHAPTER THREE

WILL WAS silent. He had lost all his ebullience, even his authority, as he turned back to stare at the *Green Lady.*

'We could rebuild her. Just sail away. All four of us,' he muttered. Then he pulled himself together and said, 'Those students. That was going too damn far.'

'I saw the wheel tracks of the photographers' car,' said Tim. 'It was – weird they were here again.'

'Why would they have anything to do with it?' said Will with an irritable edge to his voice.

'He got knocked off his bike a metre from where I reckon their car was.'

'But the Renault went hours before. I saw them drive off. They even came and thanked me for letting them use the track. Talk sense.'

Tim subsided, deflated. Then he remembered something else. 'Dino had a screwed-up bit of paper in his hand. Wouldn't let me see it.'

'Probably had some obscenity on it. Students

17

nowadays—' Will took refuge in the cliché. Then he came to life again, as if he was switching back to his old self. 'Let's go and see this red-faced son of mine.' He put his arm round Tim's shoulders and they walked back through the sunlit yard which smelt of blistered wood, tar and seaweed. 'How do you get on with Dino now?' he asked.

'All right.' Tim wondered if Will was trying to distract him.

'But not *that* well . . .'

'He's older than me.'

'He's not a bad boy. Just difficult. Never got on with his mother. Not that I did either, towards the end. Dino reckons he's cool, but he's a little kid underneath.'

Tim looked up at him sharply. He had never heard his stepfather sound so patronizing. 'Mum wants to write to the principal of the college.'

'Yeah.' Will sounded unenthusiastic.

'Isn't that a good thing?'

'Dino hands it out. He's got to take it too.'

'Red paint's a bit much, isn't it?'

'Yes.' Will was reflective again and his grip tightened on Tim's shoulder. 'It is.'

That evening, as Tim watched TV in the dining-room and did his homework at the same time, his mother came in.

18

'Now what are you doing?'

'Homework.'

'With the TV on?'

'Mum – it's all right.'

'It's not.' But her heart was obviously not in the argument. 'Look at those walls.'

'Eh?'

'Only painted three weeks ago and the damp's coming through already.'

'It's only a tiny patch.'

'Bad enough.' She hovered in the doorway and he knew she was worrying about something. Mum always hovered when she was worried.

'What is it?'

'Sorry?'

'Come on, Mum. You still upset about Dino?'

'Disgraceful. I'm writing to the principal. Whatever Will thinks.' She hesitated, staring down at the tablecloth that was stained with tomato sauce. 'Now look at that—'

'Come on, Mum. Something's on your mind.'

'You happy, love?' she asked abruptly.

'Sure.'

'It's been a lot for you to take on – these two men,' she said anxiously.

'Will's great.' He wanted to be optimistic.

'And Dino?'

'I'm getting used to him.'

19

But she was still restless, adjusting things on the sideboard, straightening a picture.

'Why don't you come to the point?' he asked, lowering the sound on the TV.

'They're out there.' She spoke awkwardly, her voice full of anxiety.

He stared at her, wondering if she meant the mysterious photographers had returned.

'Dino and Will.'

'Out where?' It was like extracting information from a reluctant prisoner.

'In the yard.' Her agitated fingers dragged part of the curtain off the runners and she began to thread it back on again.

'So?'

'Having an argument.'

'What about?'

'*I* don't know.' She turned round to face him, sounding martyred and excluded.

Tim had often wondered about the bad relationship between Will and Dino, particularly after he had overheard them in the boat-yard office. 'I don't trust you,' Dino had said. And who were Luigi and the Don? But Tim didn't want to tell his mother about the conversation he had overheard. He wasn't quite sure why, but maybe it had something to do with not stirring it up. Tim had got used to his original suspicions now and learnt to live with them. Their new life was so good. He didn't want *anything* to spoil it, but it was hard to cling on to that hope given the recent turn of events – and now this!

'Do you want me to go out there?' he asked.

'Of course not.' She looked away, studying the dust on the TV screen.

'Then—'

'Will seems more fond of you than Dino.' As she spoke, Tim realized how little they had really talked about this massive change in their lives – how they had rushed into it all, so full of hope. From that mean street in Torridge to Whispers in such a short space of time.

'Don't be daft.'

'It's true.' Now Marian had broached the subject at last, she clearly wanted to talk. 'You know how physical Will is, but he never touches Dino. And you've got interests in common. In fact, you're rather alike in some ways. That wretched Dickens – and the running. Sometimes I wonder if Dino's really happy. I know I can't reach him, and he seems so self-contained. His mother never really – not that I know anything about the woman. Maybe they were all unhappy in a—'

'Mum?' Tim interrupted her worried flow of talk.

'Yes?'

'What do you want me to *do*?'

*

21

But Tim had known all along, he thought to himself, as he hurried out of the pub and over the long, rank grass of the derelict beer garden. She had wanted him to make it all right – to prop up her own system of control. She *always* wanted *everybody* to be all right and would go to considerable lengths to attain her objective. Mum liked a quiet surface to her life, even if everything was boiling away, ready to explode underneath.

He heard the raised voices almost immediately and paused, knowing that he wanted to eavesdrop again and summoning up the moral courage to do so. Then he realized that he didn't need any moral courage, for Will and Dino were both talking in Sicilian. But by the tone of their voices, there was no doubt they were having a row. Then Tim heard a cry of pain.

He waited and then walked on into the scented night towards the boat-yard. Dino was holding on to the *Green Lady*, his hand to his mouth. This time it wasn't red paint that Tim saw.

Will was hurrying away towards the creek and the path that led away from the boat-yard to the marsh. A nightjar called repeatedly as if monitoring his progress, and a crescent moon sailed above them in a dark sky ruffled by rushing grey clouds.

'What happened?' Tim asked Dino for the second time that day.

He winced, wiping the blood from his lips. He

was angry in a smouldering, sullen way, but he also seemed beaten. Tim had never seen him this way before.

'He'll pay.'

'Will hit you?'

Dino hesitated. 'It's to do with back home,' he muttered.

'Please tell me.' Tim was desperate to make contact, and he knew that if he could there might be some kind of friendship between them. 'I want to be mates with you, Dino. What *is* going on between you and Will? Why did he hit you?'

There were still some traces of red paint in Dino's hair, making a strange contrast with the real blood on his mouth.

For a moment he hesitated. 'Owe money,' he said woodenly.

'At Orinoco's?'

'In Sicily.'

'But Mum could help . . .' Tim stopped, remembering that he didn't want her to invest any more money in his stepfather.

'Too much.'

'How much?'

Dino shrugged. 'My father – he not what you see.' His hand went to his lip.

'I don't understand.'

'No matter,' he said sharply, obviously regretting what he had just said.

'But it does.' Tim knew that he had to find out what was going on. He felt unsettled, anxious.

'Forget what I said.'

'Can't you tell me any more?'

'No.'

'Why did he hit you?'

Suddenly Dino grabbed Tim by the shoulders and he could feel the strength in the Sicilian's wrists. 'I like you. I like your mother. I *know* my father.'

'There weren't any students, were there?' The realization came to Tim, more out of instinct than anything else. 'It's something more, isn't it? Bigger.' He felt hot and panicky, not really wanting to know; it was all too much of a threat. Tim thought of his mother back in the house, dusting as she always did when she was worried. He needed to protect her, and himself. He didn't want change. After all, their new life had hardly started.

'You shut up.' Dino's grip tightened.

'And they weren't photographers either. Who were they? They looked foreign. Were they Sicilians – come to get the money he owes? What was in that note? And was the paint a warning?' The questions came tumbling out so fast that Dino looked bemused. 'Why did he hit you?' Tim persisted. He didn't want to ask about all this, but every instinct made him go babbling on.

'I told him we can't run. He knows what they're

like. Now they've found him, they won't let him go. Not again.'

'Who are they?'

Dino shook his head.

'Please tell me.'

'Men he work with.'

'What are we going to do?' Tim was beside himself with anxiety now, and he wished Dino had never told him anything – and yet he *had* to know. 'Can't we call the police?'

'No.'

'Then what *can* we do?'

'I ring my uncle.'

'He'll pay them off?'

But Dino didn't reply. 'I'm scared,' he admitted, and then pulled himself together. 'That all now. You not tell – *any* of this. If you do, my father will go.'

'But is Mum in danger?' Tim felt panic-stricken at the idea of Will departing. They had only just got together. Now there was this threat from outside which was so much worse than his original suspicions.

'No.'

'How do you make that out?'

'You ask one more question and I break your neck.' But for the first time Dino was looking at him with a hint of affection.

'Then you'll have to break my neck. She's my mother – and I care about her.'

'That's why I like you.'

'Well?'

'I speak to uncle.'

'Why didn't you do that before?'

'My father – he say no. He is proud man. Like Sicilians.'

'And how will you explain all that away?' Tim pointed at Dino's mouth, where the blood was caking.

'I will tell Marian my father tries to stop me seeing girl. I say no. He hit me. OK?'

'Sort of. It'll do – I suppose.' Tim was doubtful, but he wasn't interested in Dino's excuses. Will clearly had a past, and it was rapidly catching up with him.

As they walked back across the boat-yard, Dino put his arm round him, just as Will had done. 'You don't speak to my father about this.'

'No.'

'Our secret.'

'You don't think he'll tell me himself?'

'Too proud.'

Tim could understand that, but no doubt there were other reasons too.

'Our secret,' Dino persisted, looking at him anxiously in a rather childish way.

'OK. But you'd better get on to your uncle. Do you think he'll be able to help?'

'Yes.'

'Why did they throw the paint over you? Why didn't they chuck it over Will?'

'In my village – it is a custom.'

'What kind of custom?'

'When a father has done wrong, it is his son who has the warning. They reach him through his loved one.'

'Do you think stepsons count for that too?' asked Tim in alarm.

Dino laughed in a harsh, cracked sort of way. 'Not while I'm around,' he replied.

CHAPTER FOUR

'MEN!' MARIAN took refuge in one of her unshake-able beliefs – that only women could save the world; men simply spoilt it. It was a cliché, but Tim often thought she had a point. Dressing Dino's lip she continued to grumble, but Tim knew that she was pleased to do something, to get closer to Will's son. 'What with the paint and now this; it's not exactly a red-letter day for you, Dino.'

'Don't understand.'

'Just an English expression. As for that father of yours – I'll give him what for when he gets in. Tim!'

'Yes, Mum?'

'Turn the telly off and get on with that homework.'

'OK.'

'Now, why did your father hit you?'

'I insult him.'

'That's no reason for violence.' She worked the Savlon into his split lip with enthusiasm.

She's an innocent, thought Tim. And then more darkly – she mustn't be hurt. Not ever.

'What did you say to him?' she asked curiously.

'I say he not interfere in my life. With girls.'

'Oh, them,' she replied, as if she was talking about a remote and rather unattractive tribe.

Will was subdued when he returned, and when Marian tore into him, he put up no defence at all. Because he didn't want to be around, Tim slipped up to bed and thought about what Dino had told him. Basically it came down to the fact that Will had owed a considerable sum of money in Sicily and had done a runner. For some reason, Dino had come with him. For English girls? That seemed unlikely. The two so-called photographers in the Renault were clearly Sicilian and had had Whispers under surveillance. What were they doing? Evaluating the property to pay off Will's debts? They then threw paint over Dino and drove off, presumably leaving a note for his father – a threatening note demanding the return of the debt.

The paint was a warning. Could it mean that next time the paint would be blood – blood for the father, paint for the son? And what about the regular late night telephone calls that now seemed to have stopped? 'I don't trust you.' Dino's voice rang in his ears. If Will didn't pay his debts, which

29

Tim was sure he couldn't, how far would the two men go? Was Mum in danger? And himself? It was a chilling thought. But there were other mysteries. For instance, why had Dino forbidden him to talk to Will? And should he break his promise? With his mother at risk, Tim suddenly resolved that he would, but, as he drifted into uneasy sleep, he thought of life without his stepfather. With some amazement he realized that if Will left, life would become unbearable. Tim tried to reason it out. At the beginning he had been suspicious of him; now he was even more so – but there was an overriding factor that he had not realized before. He loved him.

'Tim?'
  'Mm?'
  'You asleep?'
  'What?'
  'It's Will.' He sat down on the bed beside Tim in the darkness. 'I only wanted to say goodnight.' His voice was soft and warm and loving, but there was something else to it – an edge, as if every word counted.

Blearily, Tim wondered if he was over-reacting, making it up. He just wanted the new start to continue and to build up stability. They all needed a hopeful present and a promising future. What they didn't want was the past to reach out to them, either from Torridge or Sicily.

The past. Tim saw it as a black dog stalking them on the marshes, giving a few warning howls, biding its time to sink its teeth into the temporary security they had all found.

'And there's something else.' His stepfather's voice shook a little.

'What?'

'I wanted to say how much I love my new family, and I'm determined to prove myself to you and your mother. It'll take time but I will – whatever happens.'

'What do you mean – whatever happens?' asked Tim fearfully.

Will shrugged in the darkness.

'What *is* going to happen?'

'Nothing.'

'Then—'

'Remember I love you. Always remember that.'

Tim was surprised for he had never heard his stepfather speak so emotionally before.

'I realize we haven't been together long.' It was as if he was trying to pre-empt Tim's thoughts. 'But you must remember how wonderful it is for me to have a new family and a place in it for Dino. I tell you – we're going somewhere. I promise you that. I won't let you down.'

'I know you won't.' But Tim knew he sounded

as if he was giving his stepfather a warning rather than an affirmation. Now why was he doing that? Tim could see that Will was perceptive enough to register his tone and yet he carried on, switching to a kind of boyish enthusiasm that didn't quite come off.

'You *wait* till you see Whispers in a few months time. That bar I used to have in Fortuna really worked – I must show it to you some day.' He laughed. 'We'll pass over the Orinoco. That could be classified as *any* port in a storm.' He paused. 'Anyway, Tim. God bless you.' He got up and went over to the door. 'Believe in me,' he half whispered, the boyishness gone.

'You bet,' Tim assured him, but he was still uneasy.

Tim woke later that night to what he initially thought was the sound of a gun shot. Then he dismissed the idea. It had to be a car backfiring. But why here? Then he heard his mother's voice and jumped out of bed, pulled on his dressing gown and slippers and raced into the living room. He found her with the window open, staring out into the overgrown garden. She was shaking.

'Mum?'

'I can't see. I can't see what's going on.'

'Where's Will?'

'I don't know. There was this noise. I think it was a car. I couldn't see, but that Renault's here again – you can just make it out.'

He could – a dark shadow on the track in the harsh moonlight. There was no doubt they weren't out for photographs at this time of night, but what *did* they want? His stepfather's voice crept into his mind. 'Believe in me.'

'Will went to the window about half an hour ago. Then he said he thought he'd left the back door unlocked,' said Marian.

'He didn't come back?' Blood for the father. Paint for the son. The chant was like some macabre nursery rhyme.

'I wasn't worried. He sometimes gets up in the night and has a whisky. He hasn't been sleeping recently.'

'I'm going down.' Tim was adamant.

'No—'

She made a grab at him, but he slipped out of her grasp and ran lightly down the stairs. His mother followed.

'Wait.'

'I've got to get out there.'

'I *said* – wait.'

She held his arm and hung on to him as they struggled in front of the open back door until he managed to wrench himself free again, dashing out into the yard. There was no one around, but then

Tim thought he heard someone moving in the old barrel store. So far he had not had time to feel afraid, but the words bit into his mind again. Blood for the father. Paint for the son.

Slowly, cautiously, he walked towards the store, knowing his mother would not be far behind. He paused for a moment in the total silence of the moonlit yard. Old beer barrels, steel casks, scattered crates lay in long, ragged grass, while the rusting wreck of an old van, broken fencing and an enamel bath lay on the track that led round the back to the garage and eventually the marsh.

Again he heard a noise and he was sure that it was coming from the store. Where was Mum? Where were Will and Dino? Could someone be hurt in there?

Tim inched open the door and crept in, but he had no torch and the inside was pitch black. Then he heard an engine being revved hard.

The Renault swept into the yard with its headlights blazing and Tim crouched by the window. Suddenly he heard a little moan behind him. There was only one way out and that was back into the yard, but before he could make a decision a car door slammed and he heard footsteps. Then a torch beam swept the interior.

Slumped against some cardboard boxes, Tim could now see the young man he had noticed before in the Renault. Blood, a bright red stream looking theatrical and unreal, oozed through a hole in his jacket sleeve.

Then a voice whispered, 'Giuseppe. It's Pietro.'

The young man staggered to his feet and the penetrating beam caught Tim. He shrank away as something gleamed in the pallid light. A gun.

Holding the gun was the elderly man from the Renault. He was distinctive-looking at close range, with his swept-back white hair and tanned, almost leathery skin. Tim began to shake, a cold sweat breaking out on his body, sure that they were going to kill him. He watched Giuseppe leaning on a cask, making little moaning sounds that he was trying to suppress – but couldn't. With a sinking heart, Tim realized they must both be Sicilians.

'Your stepfather is dangerous,' Pietro said angrily, and Tim could now see that he was sweating too. 'Do you understand?'

Tim said nothing. His entire world – and all its logic – suddenly seemed to have been blown apart.

Pietro took Giuseppe in his arms and tried to hold him upright. 'I don't know what William has told you, but whatever it is – it's a lie.'

'Who are you?' asked Tim woodenly, his throat so dry that he could hardly bring the words out.

'We are people who are owed money. But you must help me with Giuseppe. Before your stepfather gets back.' With a considerable rush of relief Tim realized that he was not a target, but outside he could hear his mother calling and felt an instant stab of fear for her.

'Please,' Giuseppe spoke for the first time. 'You do not understand. William has – has our employer's money.'

'Will hasn't *got* any money.' Tim stared at them in complete bewilderment. His feelings had changed from terror to incomprehension.

'It is in a British bank account,' Pietro insisted. 'We want it back.'

'But that's crazy. He hasn't got any money,' Tim repeated. 'My *mother* bought this place.' He wasn't afraid now – just angry and defensive. The men were obviously lying. They *had* to be.

'Please help get Giuseppe into the car. He needs treatment. I can't manage him myself.'

'What's wrong with him?'

'Your stepfather shot him.'

Tim was incredulous. 'He wouldn't do that.'

Pietro ignored him. 'Giuseppe is losing much blood. You help.' One arm around Giuseppe, he turned the gun towards Tim but his hand was unsteady.

By now confused and not knowing who to believe, Tim numbly grabbed at Giuseppe and together they half pulled, half dragged him to the Renault.

Once he was inside, sprawled across the rear

36

seat, Pietro turned back to Tim and said, 'You don't let William stay. He's no good.'

Tim darted a glance around the yard. 'Where is he?'

'Looking for me.'

'He's out on the marsh?'

'Yes.'

'I didn't even know he'd *got* a gun.' Tim was still unable to take in all the implications of what had happened.

'William likes to punish those who love him.'

'Love?'

'So I have punished *him*.' Pietro's voice broke and a feeling of dread seized Tim. That was why Will didn't come. He was dead. Blood for the father.

'What are you saying?' Tim half whispered. 'You haven't – hurt Will?'

'He deserves all he gets.' Pietro got into the car, slammed the door and switched on the ignition as Tim ran over, beating at the window of the Renault with his fists.

'Where is he?' he yelled. 'You've got to tell me where my stepfather is. You've got to tell me if he's hurt.'

Pietro simply drove out of the yard.

Tim chased after him, something twisting in his heart. Now he knew how much he really loved Will.

'Are you all right?' Tim's mother was standing by the car park fence looking utterly defenceless, and he hurried over, throwing his arms around her, trying to hold back his tears. 'I've been searching for you everywhere – who were they?'

'Those so-called photographers.'

'Them! What were they doing? And where are Will and Dino?'

For some reason, Tim hesitated. Although he knew he should tell her everything, he had a sudden reservation. Dino had made an allegation about Will and so had Pietro. They could both have been lying. Either way, once again he didn't want to worry her. Not yet. The boat had been rocked hard enough. Believe in me, Will had said, and Tim wanted to do just that. But where *was* his stepfather? Was he alive or—

'Did they see you?'

'No. I was hiding in the store.' Could she have seen him helping Giuseppe out? Then he told himself it was unlikely; the building was on the corner and well away from the fence. 'I just saw two men run in and drive off. One of them had a gun.'

'So I *did* hear shooting. For God's sake, Tim – what's happening? Red paint and now this—'

'Will and Dino are on the marsh, I think,' replied Tim, trying to recover some self-control so that he could sound reasonably reassuring. 'They must be searching for those men. Let's go and find them.'

He was so desperate to find out what had happened to Will he would have liked to run off, but he knew he had to wait for her. What had Pietro meant when he said his stepfather liked to punish 'those who love him'?

Suddenly they heard the sound of running feet.

'Someone's coming,' said Tim fearfully.

As they paused uncertainly by the store. Dino came running up the path from the creek.

'Where's Will?' yelled Marian.

'Those guys got him.' He was so much out of breath that he could hardly speak.

'What do you mean – *got* him?' demanded Tim, the sweat running into his eyes and the panic surging through him like an icy wave.

'Shot in leg.'

'Where is he?' Marian was beside herself with shock and fury and frustration. 'Where the hell *is* he?'

'We'll have to carry him,' said Dino. 'He can't stand.'

An incredibly ironic picture suddenly surfaced in Tim's mind. They would get Will into casualty – only to meet Giuseppe. He swallowed a burst of almost hysterical laughter, but his mother was already stumbling back towards the track. Dino and Tim followed.

'He'll be all right, Mum.'

'How do you *know* that? I love him. I love him so much.'

'So do I,' he replied.

They ran together, desperate to reach the stranger they had both begun to care for so much.

CHAPTER FIVE

WHEN TIM and his mother found Will, he was lying in a hollow behind one of the dykes with his face twisted in pain and his leg splayed out. The dawn was a grey slash in the sky and in the near darkness, Tim could hear his stepfather's heavy breathing.

'How bad?' Marian asked, plummeting down beside him, capable as she always was in a crisis.

'Just a flesh wound.'

'Why did they *do* it?' She was still distraught, but her shock was dispersing into a general sense of outrage and indignation.

'They're debt collectors.'

'With guns?'

'I owe them.'

'You didn't tell me.'

'Why should I?' he replied miserably. 'I was trying to make a fresh start – and I'm still going to. You know that.'

Then Mum came into her own and Tim felt a surge of great love for her. She might like her fun, she might panic and nag, but she was brilliant at making decisions. When everyone else was indecisive, she always asserted herself. Tim had seen it happen so many times before – when she changed her job, sorted out a teacher at the primary school, decided to take out a bank loan for a new car. And now, with Will lying wounded beside her as if he was an actor in a gangster film, she said firmly, 'And that new start's staying put. How much do you owe them?'

'Too much.'

'*Come* on!'

'Forty grand.'

'I'll pay it.'

'You can't.'

'Why not?' She glared down at him. 'I've got enough.'

'We need it for Whispers.'

'You can still have it. The money will just about stretch. And if it's forty grand that's at stake—'

Will nodded.

'How on earth did you run up a debt like that?'

'I borrowed money to take out a lease on a restaurant in Fortuna – next door to the bar. I wanted to set Dino up.'

'At his age?'

'I had a chef. It was an investment for the future. But I was inexperienced, the chef was hopeless and the place got a lousy reputation. We closed with the lease still to run and there was a hefty penalty clause. My marriage was over, I couldn't pay back the debt – so Dino and I did a bunk. And that's all there is to my mysterious past.'

Pietro and Giuseppe *must* have been lying, thought Tim. Their story was so bizarre. And he *had* to believe his stepfather or his world would be empty again. They might even have to go back to Torridge! He and Mum would never be able to cope with Whispers on their own. Tim knew he was taking a risk, but he had begun to live a day at a time.

'I'll suggest I pay the money back over a period of time,' Will was saying.

'After what's happened?' Marian snapped.

'They just put the frighteners on me. The red paint on Dino, and now this.'

'Is *that* all?'

'Yes – that's all.'

But Marian was determined not to let him get away with such a glib statement. 'A gun may be an essential everyday domestic convenience in Sicily, but not here—'

And where's yours, Will? Tim wondered. Is Dino looking after it for you?

'My father owned restaurant that failed and he insulted people who lend him money. That is important in Sicily. That is a bad debt.' Dino was clearly wanting to back him up, but Will merely looked irritated.

'Who *are* these people?' Marian demanded. 'What sort of villains would send armed men to recover a loan?'

'They're family,' said Will hesitantly.

'Whose family?' she asked.

'You don't understand. Cosa Nostra.'

'Sorry?' Marian was completely bewildered now.

'Mafia,' said Tim. 'He's talking about the Mafia.'

CHAPTER SIX

'THE MAFIA? Here?' Marian stared at Tim as if he had made a stupid joke, and then looked blankly at Will.

He nodded apologetically, as if explaining away a disagreement with the Inland Revenue.

But you're mixed up in a lot more, aren't you? Tim thought to himself, unable to really go along with what his stepfather was saying. On one level he daren't even think of losing all they had with Will; on another, he was still deeply suspicious. The two sets of thoughts were painful in the extreme. He was now sure Will was admitting just so much but still putting up a smoke-screen. The questions went round and round in his mind. You have a gun – and you shot Giuseppe. Was that just self-defence? Did they really come as debt collectors, or was there another motive? Maybe Will's lies were so multi-layered that the only way to learn the truth was to give him enough rope to hang himself.

Tim suddenly felt sick as he faced a reality which

he did not understand and wished he didn't feel so confused. After all, despite his so-called explanations, they knew nothing of Will's past. He could be a con-man, could be involved in serious crime. If Pietro was telling the truth, why was Will keeping money in a bank account and deceiving Mum – making her pay out even more? Was he simply using her? The questions continued to pound in Tim's head, giving him a blinding headache.

Meanwhile, Marian was helping Dino to lift Will to his feet with his arms around their shoulders.

'You've *got* to go to hospital.' She was insistent.

'I can't,' Will pleaded. 'If the police get involved in this—'

Dino smoothly interceded. 'He's right. If the police interview – much trouble.'

'How's that?' Marian asked suspiciously as they began to half carry Will, as he hopped along on his good leg.

'Sicilian trouble,' Dino said vaguely.

Marian hesitated. She didn't want to make matters worse. 'So what are we going to do?' she asked.

'I have to take the money to Sicily in person,' said Will. 'This is a debt of honour, and I have to apologize. It's not good enough to sign a cheque.' He sounded melodramatic and Tim found it hard to believe him. So did Marian.

'Let's get you into bed first. Then we'll talk about this crazy stunt.' She sounded brisk and reproving, as if she was dealing with a pair of troublesome kids.

Will lay back on the double bed that dominated the small room in the eaves of the pub. Marian sat on a chair beside him, dressing the flesh wound just above his knee. After all Tim's fears it was only a nick, but was still bleeding slightly. Dino and Tim sat on the end of the bed. Mum's in charge, he thought proudly; Will's helpless – and this is the third time today she's patched someone up. She was getting to be like a district nurse.

'Why do you need to take this money to Sicily?' Marian asked hesitantly, considering the idea seriously now.

'A Sicilian businessman loaned me the money to set up the restaurant. I can't give you his name.'

'Why not?' she asked irritably.

'Because it's better for you to know as little as possible, and it doesn't help you to know his name. But I assure you he's a man of honour and if I give him the money in person, he'll respect me again.' Will sounded rather more convincing now. That's the trouble though, thought Tim. We *want* to believe him.

'And kill you?' asked Marian.

Will shook his head. 'That's not the way it works.'

'He's right,' added Dino.

'Who is this man?' she persisted. 'Is he a member of the Mafia as well?' She kept alternating between anxiety and derision.

'Yes,' replied Will. 'But Sicilian business dealings don't just mean violence and vendettas – that's an old movie cliché. They're far more subtle than that, I can assure you. I borrowed money from an important man and ratted on him, and I should have realized the consequences. Now I have to go back and make my peace with him – hand over the money personally with a profound apology. You *have* to understand.'

'If you're going to Sicily, I'm coming with you,' Marian replied, with surprising vigour and authority.

'Of course you can't,' said Will as if she had proposed a journey to Mars.

'So am I,' Tim added quickly, and was even more surprised that his mother didn't raise any immediate objection. He thought she would refuse point-blank to let him go at all, but as usual he had underestimated her desire to weld them all together, to keep her new life from being dispersed.

'You say he's a man of honour, that no harm can come to us if you repay the debt, so Tim and I are quite safe, aren't we?' She didn't sound

48

convinced, and for the first time he realized the extent of his mother's love for Will; she obviously felt so much for him that she was actually prepared to expose them both to the dangers of going to a place famous for its violent reputation. He wondered if she would back out later, but in his experience this was unlikely. Once she had made up her mind she always stuck to it – something she called 'seeing it through' or 'backing her hunches'. That had applied to her job, the way she had coped with his father's walk-out, the decision to move to Whispers. Now she was preparing to meet the Mafia. What a mother, he thought. And then – almost at the same time – what a risk. Tim felt a twinge of self-pity. Did she love Will more than him? Shouldn't she be more protective?

'You must *not* come,' Dino interrupted, trying to be forceful and failing.

'Rubbish.' Marian swept on, focusing her attention on Will. 'If I don't come – then I won't put up the money. We're a family now, but we haven't got much history. We bought Whispers together, we'll go to Sicily together – Tim as well – that's the *only* way it's going to work.' She paused and then said quickly, but with considerable determination, 'I don't know what the hell's in your past, Will, and I can't even guess at how much you're hiding from me.'

49

'I'm hiding nothing—' he began, but Marian swept on.

'But whatever it is – we'll share it with you. I've lost one man and I'm not going to lose another. So it's all or nothing, Will. And it had better *be* all—'

'Of course it is,' he began weakly.

'Or I'll think you're just after my money,' she finished challengingly.

His stepfather nodded, looking as amazed as Tim. The fact that she was actually coming – and bringing her son with her – seemed to have silenced him completely. Tim almost smiled to himself. Was Will really naïve enough to think she would let him take her money to Sicily on his own – or even with Dino? Then he wondered if she was hanging on to a straw in the wind. That was a phrase that might well describe Will Benson.

'OK.' Will spoke slowly. 'Nobody will harm you.'

He sounded as if he was acting a part in a second-rate film. Then the seriousness of the situation struck Tim again. Will *might* be repaying a so-called debt of honour, but by withholding the information he had, surely Tim was putting his mother and himself into terrible danger. Shouldn't he be more responsible? Yet there was something else to be balanced against all this. He knew he loved Will now and so did Mum. Tim didn't want to run the risk of driving Will away for ever by voicing his distrust.

'Do you love me, Will?' Marian asked quietly.

'You know I do.'

'Really?' She took his hand and Tim felt excluded, isolated, uncertain.

Will sat up, wincing with pain. 'I'm trying to make a new start, Marian. I've got to and so has Dino. You *have* to trust me. You'll both be safe – you have my word. And when we get back, we can finally put the past behind us. I'll never let you down.'

They smiled at each other rather uncertainly, and as she put a large plaster over the wound, Marian said, 'I had no idea when I married you that we were going to end up with a redundant pub, a closed-down boat-yard, a forty grand debt and a wild west shoot-out. It's a bit rich, isn't it?'

Will nodded and winced again as she pressed the plaster down firmly. 'Rich it certainly is.' He grinned in his disarming way and then looked serious.

You're acting, Tim thought. You're acting and you're lying, but I'm so fond of you and maybe, like Mum, I'd follow you to the ends of the earth. He thought of life as it had been before Will and Dino had arrived. Torridge. The loneliness. The squalid street and the horrible house with Mum always seeming to be at work. Mum always tired.

Will might be a rogue but he had revitalized them both, and Tim would rather go anywhere with him than return to the mean streets of Torridge. Of course he had to remind himself that even if Will did push off, they would still have Mum's money – and probably much more if they didn't have to pay off his stepfather's debts – but then they wouldn't be a family. That had become the most important thing. So Tim finally decided there and then to keep to himself what Pietro had told him. They must all stick together and nothing must be allowed to come between them.

'Will?' He was hesitant.

'Yes, Tim?'

'If you don't pay this debt back, will they send someone to kill you?'

'Yes.'

'Couldn't we move?'

'Give up Whispers?' He was almost comical in his childish indignation. 'You must be out of your mind – and who wants to spend their life in hiding? I mean – I'm sorry it's out of your Mum's money and I do realize it's a big chunk, but when we get back I'll go on slaving at this place, doing my best to make it a paying proposition.'

Tim knew that he would. Even if the business failed and he had to be bailed out again, there could be no doubt that Will was a phenomenally hard worker.

'Who is this family?' he asked. 'Who's in the Cosa Nostra?'

'I've told you that.'

'I mean – who are they as people?' Tim persisted, determined to know more. Was Luigi – the man Will had been speaking to on the phone – was he part of the Cosa Nostra too? But Tim didn't want to interrupt the flow, to say how much he knew. Not now.

'I owe the money to Raphael Carlotti,' said Will reluctantly. 'He's a wealthy man. He owns a number of charter yachts, but his main income comes from his property investment. In certain ways, most ways, he's a good man. An honourable man.'

'An honourable man who sends out debt collectors with guns?' asked Tim calmly, wondering how much information he could squeeze out of his stepfather.

'I betrayed him,' said Will. 'In other words, I did a runner with Dino here. I was a fool.'

'He'd try to kill you for forty grand?' Marian was scoffing. 'A rich man like that?' She was playing the devil's advocate now.

'It's a debt,' said Dino.

'So he'd send out assassins for 50p?' asked Tim. He no longer felt like a child. He was an adult, trying to hack his way into a conspiracy. It was a strangely exciting feeling.

'Neither of you understands what a debt of honour means,' said Will. 'I ran off after he had been good to me. Believed in me. That's why he sent out his debt collectors. But they're not assassins.'

'What are they then?'

'They were sent to punish me, and extract a promise to pay up in person. To hand the money in cash to Carlotti.'

'He really won't harm anyone,' Dino explained. 'You've got to believe that.'

'What's more,' said Will, 'I wouldn't put you at risk. If I thought there was any chance of that, I'd insist on going alone.'

'We wouldn't let you.' Marian was firm.

'We're all in this together.' Tim might now have a voice amongst the adults, but he also realized that, like his stepfather, he was withholding vital information in a desperate attempt to paper over the cracks.

'That's family,' muttered Will.

'Yes.' Marian laughed bitterly. '*Real* family. Not your Cosa Nostra.'

CHAPTER SEVEN

WHERE HAS Will hidden his gun? wondered Tim as he lay awake during what was left of the night. He spent hours tossing and turning, mulling over the situation, but came to no definite conclusion – except that he was sure his stepfather was sticking to his own heavily protected version of the truth.

Then, as he drifted off to sleep, Tim remembered again how companionable Will had been, how much of a father he already was to him. Those early mornings with the mist rising over the creek and the long grass moist with dew as they jogged along the dykes. There was just room for them to run side by side, their breathing matching their stride in almost exact synchronization. They always sat down on the other side of Whispers where they could see the tall spire of a church rising needle-like from the flat marshes. An old hulk of a barge lay rotting in the mud, just spars now. They often talked about Dickens' novel *Great Expectations* – the one they both enjoyed more than any other. Will could go on almost obsessively about the convicts who were imprisoned on the barges on the River Thames, and Tim had felt excited by his stepfather's ability to step into a world of fiction and close the door behind him.

'You know, Tim,' he had once said, 'if it weren't for books I'd go barmy. There would be nowhere to hide – and to *really* live.'

Now, as he lay there, Tim heard him say it again and again; he had suddenly understood that Will needed to shelter in fiction and in his imagination more than he had ever realized. Mum was right, Tim did have a good deal in common with his stepfather. They both found shelter from the grim realities of life in reading and running. Here they had a real bond, and whatever Will had done – or was doing – nothing could take that away. But what was fact in his stepfather's life, and what was fiction? Did even Will know?

The next day was Saturday, and although Tim woke early feeling exhausted, he decided to go for a run by the side of the creek to clear his head – and to try and think. He put on a track suit and hurried downstairs to find his mother in the kitchen making coffee.

'You up already? I thought you'd stay in bed and catch up.'

'Couldn't sleep.'

'Neither could I.' She turned to him and smiled. Suddenly Tim realized that it was a while since they had been alone together for any length of time.

'I was going out for a run.'

'Have a cup of coffee with me first.'

'OK.'

Tim sat up on one of the kitchen stools and held the hot mug in his hand. The coffee was dark and strong and soothing.

'Do you believe him?' she asked.

A twinge of conscience twisted inside him. He should immediately tell her what Pietro had said, but if he did, it was very unlikely they would ever know the truth. Tim sternly told himself that he mustn't give in to the constant temptation to confide in her. His stepfather had to be tested – not thrown out. It would be self-indulgent of him to make her more concerned – to make her doubt Will even more profoundly.

'Sort of.'

'That's the way I feel. Do you reckon I married a villain?' She grinned, but Tim knew his mother was desperate for his opinion.

'A bit of a one. But he's a good guy really,' he said rather weakly.

'How do you know that?'

'I can feel it inside.' Tim wanted to believe what he was saying – and almost did so. He realized

57

ruefully that this might be yet another link with his stepfather.

'That's what I've got – gut reaction,' his mother agreed. 'That's why I fell in love with Will in the first place. So what are we going to do?'

'Go.'

'To Sicily. And fight the Mafia?' She laughed.

'I don't think they're *quite* the same as in the movies. Do you?'

'Not really. I just can't understand why Will got himself into such trouble – why he ran off like that.'

'He's an adventurer.' That was something Tim was *really* certain about.

'Maybe. But it sometimes worries me – knowing so little about him. He never talks to me about his ex-wife – perhaps that's fair enough, but neither does Dino. It's a different world.'

'Do you think that's another reason for him agreeing to take us there?' Tim asked.

'I wondered about that – whether it would be easier to explain it all if we were actually in Sicily.' She sounded hopeful.

'He should do. You're paying enough for it,' said Tim.

She sighed. 'I know. But I love him – and I don't think I'm being conned. OK, so he's made one hell of a mess of everything, but you're right, he's *not* a villain. Not through and through. I know he's not.' Then she stared at Tim intently. 'I want to believe in him – until I can't any longer. Is that OK?'

'Yes,' he said, relieved. It was exactly what he had wanted to hear.

The sun was climbing into a brilliant cobalt sky as Tim ran along the dykes that separated the creek from the marsh. As he sped away from Whispers, much of his exhaustion eased in a rush of optimism. There was no doubt about it – Will was offering them the adventure of a lifetime, despite its dubious overtones.

But a little later, running through the longer grass beside the marsh, Tim's spirits fell, and as he passed the hollow where they had found Will he stopped and sat down to think. There was a small object lying in the grass by his foot and he leant over and picked it up.

A bullet. As he ran on, the cold reality of his stepfather's life began to crowd in on him. This wasn't a game.

'Hey!'

Dino was sitting under the dyke, staring out at the muddy creek. There was only a trickle of water now, but the tide would soon be coming in.

'You like running.'

'Makes me feel good.' Tim sat down beside him. 'What are you doing out here?'

'Thinking.'

'What about?'

'Last night.'

'It was nasty,' said Tim.

'Sure.'

'So you think we shouldn't go to Sicily – that it's too risky?' Tim tried to lead him on.

'You have to go,' said Dino. 'He need Marian. He need you. My father has great hurt. You love him?'

'Yes,' he replied without hesitation.

'And your mother?'

'I know she does.' Tim had never seen Dino so anxious. 'But I'm worried that – that he just wants her for the money.'

'That is natural.'

Tim stared at him hopefully, wondering if Dino would tell him any more. He knew he was lying, that he didn't trust his own father, that they were both playing games. What was more, the rules kept changing, the goalposts kept moving. Could Dino and he ever share their love for Will, or were they going to listen to each other's lies until Doomsday?

'I'd like to trust him,' said Tim sadly. 'But I can't.' He got to his feet, wondering if Dino might say, 'Neither do I,' but he remained silent. 'I'm going to run on for a while. Do you want to come?' asked Tim impatiently.

'Me?' Dino looked horrified.

'Don't you ever run?'

'No,' he replied with a look of distaste. 'I do not see why I should *ever* have to do that.'

Maybe you've done too much running already, thought Tim.

CHAPTER EIGHT

'COME IN and have a chat.' Will was lying against a pile of plumped-up pillows.

Tim went in cautiously, realizing that even when lying flat his stepfather somehow had him at a disadvantage. He sat gingerly on the edge of the bed.

'Sorry.'

'About last night?' Tim asked.

'And everything else. I got myself mixed up in something I couldn't handle.'

'In Sicily?'

'Yeah. Didn't think Carlotti would reach me over here. Should have known better.' He paused and gave Tim a probing look. 'What did you get up to last night?'

'I came down.'

'You heard shots?'

'They woke me. Mum followed. We hunted for you – then Dino came running.'

'You didn't see any of those guys?'

'No.'

'They didn't speak to you?'

'Not a chance. I was all over the place, looking for you, trying to take care of Mum—' Tim didn't like lying but he felt he *had* to be cautious. What was Will hoping to find out? Did he suspect that Pietro had spilt the beans? If those *were* the beans.

'Good for you.'

There was a silence which Tim made no attempt to break.

'So you're sure?'

'Sure?'

'You didn't see anyone.'

'Just heard the shots.'

'OK.' Will seemed to have finally decided to believe him. 'About the Sicily trip.'

'What about it?' Tim had the curious feeling that their roles had reversed and that he was calling the shots.

'You've got to realize that Carlotti is a man of honour.'

'So you said.'

'A friend I let down.'

'Some friend.'

'It's their way. You just have to accept that, Tim. It's a different culture.' Will was clearly determined to push the point home.

'You bet it is. I still don't see why you can't send the debt back by post.'

'That would be an insult.'

'Why?'

'Because he needs to forgive me. And I want you to meet him.'

Will was beginning to sound phoney again.

'Sounds an excellent guy. He tries to kill you – you pay him back – he forgives you. What d'you make of that?' asked Tim acidly.

'It's their way. Their law. Anyway he didn't try to kill me. Merely to wound and to warn.'

'Yeah—'

'There's something else we have to talk about.'

'Well?'

'Your mother's lending me the money.'

'I know that.'

'Doesn't make you suspicious, does it?'

'What do you mean?' Tim led him on like he'd tried to do with Dino. He was getting as devious as his stepfather.

'Stop playing games.' Will frowned. 'Do you think I'm some kind of con-man?'

'I hope you're not – because I like you,' said Tim frankly and was touched to see that Will seemed genuinely moved.

'Come here.' Will grabbed his wrist. 'I'm very fond of you too, Tim. You know that. No harm's going to come to anyone. We'll go to Sicily, you'll meet Carlotti – and then we'll come back here and get on with the job. I'll pay your mum back by building up a thriving little business.'

'Nice little earner?' Tim grinned.

'You could put it that way. We're a team, us four, and we're going to win. And – don't forget what I said. Believe in me. Please believe in me.' But this time the words seemed empty.

Marian walked into the bedroom. 'What are you doing?' she asked sardonically. 'Enrolling my son into the Mafia?'

Will looked put out. He liked to tell the jokes, not listen to them.

'Tim,' he said, 'are you still re-reading *Great Expectations*?'

'Yes.'

'You want to read to me for a while?' Will smiled wryly.

'OK.'

'Bit about Joe – near the beginning.'

Marian came over and kissed Will on the forehead. 'You're just a big soft kid,' she said, but Tim knew that his stepfather wanted to shut out the world again.

Later, Tim went for a walk by the creek and then, consumed by exhaustion, lay down where Dino had sat. The tide was draining now, exposing the mud and the grey spars of an old fishing boat. Gulls swooped low, calling and searching for food, while a cormorant sat for a while on the opposite bank, staring at him enquiringly.

He glanced back at the tumbledown sheds and broken jetties, the run-down outbuildings and the tiled roof of the shabby old pub. He didn't want to go to Sicily and face all its uncertainties. Tim wanted to stay here with Will and Mum and Dino. His stepfather had said they were a team, and certainly that's what they had become as all four of them had worked so hard on renovating Whispers, where the present was the only time that mattered – not that black dog of a past.

He heard a bark and glanced around. The Alsation seemed to leap out of the very creek itself and bound towards him, its teeth bared. Then he heard its owner calling – a real naturalist this time, with field glasses and walking boots – and obediently the dog ran back.

Tim stared down at the water again, watching it gradually drain away until only pools and lagoons were left. He suddenly had the strange idea that the tide was leaving for mysterious Sicily and with it all the strength of their unity. The thought was depressing, and eventually Tim stood up and began to walk back towards the dereliction of Whispers.

CHAPTER NINE

TIM HAD never been on a plane before and felt horribly disorientated. He deeply regretted leaving home, and although he was glad to miss a few days of school, neither he nor Mum had been able to pin Will down and discover how long they would be away. He had muttered something about 'a few days – no more', but it was disconcerting. It had been even more disconcerting seeing Mum draw such a large amount of money out of the bank. The manager had queried the 'advisability of such an action', but she had blandly told him that she was buying a small villa in Spain from a local builder who wanted to be paid in sterling. The manager was even more doubtful, warning her about 'cowboys'. 'I told him I was married to one,' she later recounted to Tim.

Now, as they sat in the Boeing, he knew that Will had got the cash on him and didn't seem in the least worried about customs. Eventually, when they were having the airline's miniature and unappetizing lunch, Tim heard him saying to Marian,

'Stop worrying about the money. You know we'll be met.'

'I wish you'd tell me who by,' she complained.

'Someone who's discreet, so stop worrying. I promise you it's going to be all right.'

'You and your promises!'

'Have I broken any?'

'Hundreds.'

'Name them.'

'Can't be bothered.'

Marian kissed Will and Tim's hopes rose. Maybe it was going to be all right after all. Perhaps he shouldn't be so pessimistic. But then he realized that pessimism was perhaps the only factor he could hang on to.

He watched the clouds, densely fluffy and white, covering the sea below, occasionally shifting to reveal the vast grey-green expanse of rolling waves.

Dino woke and yawned blearily. 'We there?'

'Another half an hour.'

'Good.'

He was about to lay his dark, glossy head on the seat-back again, when Tim said, 'Tell me about Sicily.'

Dino groaned.

'You've been asleep all the flight,' said Tim indignantly.

Dino sighed. 'I tell you about the village.'

'OK.'

'It is called Corvo.' Suddenly Dino was more animated, seeing the place in his mind's eye, and as he talked Tim saw how much Dino loved his home. 'Small place with square and church. A stream that dries in summer and a path goes to top of mountain and shrine. On Saints' days, priest and choir climb carrying cross. That's tough. I know – I used to carry. There's a shop, a bar where men go, and petrol pump. It is my birth place. Up the mountain is Don Carlotti's house. The patron of Corvo.'

'Is his house posh?'

'Sure. Courtyard with fountain looks over valley.'

'Does he have a Porsche?'

'BMW.' Dino grinned.

'And you've known him all your life?'

'Yes.'

Trying not to probe too hard but unable to let the subject rest, Tim asked, 'Is he the most powerful man around?'

'There are more,' said Dino. 'Corvo torn by vendettas.'

'What are they?'

'Disputes between Don Carlotti and Don Vinci. They children together, grow up in Corvo. Cousins.'

'I don't understand.'

'It's to do with honour,' said Dino passionately

69

and Tim was surprised to see the change in him – as if he was really going home, becoming his real self at last. There was an edge to him. 'Honour is important in Sicily. You care nothing for it in England.'

'And Will has always worked just for Don Carlotti?' asked Tim, continuing to probe.

'Sure.'

'Do they live near each other?' Tim was curious about the lives of these two powerful men. He imagined them as children, fighting as children, and then fighting in a different way as adults. And what was all this about honour? It seemed important, but Tim didn't really understand why.

'Don Carlotti – his house is half-way up mountain. Don Vinci is in valley.'

'Who's going to win?' persisted Tim.

For a long time Dino didn't reply and simply closed his eyes against the questioning. Then he opened them again and gave Tim a look that meant he would tell him a little more – but not much more – and he would have to be content with that. 'Don Carlotti will win. Don Vinci – he is weak. How do you say? His time runs out. He must leave. His business – it is in trouble.'

'Where could he go?'

'France. Or Italy. Or America.'

'Shall we meet Don Carlotti? Tonight?'

'Yes.'

'What kind of man is *he*?'

'I stop now. You ask too much.'

'There isn't time to sleep,' Tim pleaded. 'We'll be landing soon. Just tell me a *bit* more.'

'Don Carlotti – he is good man, good and kind. Help village, but he is man of honour. Loans must be repaid.'

'And Don Vinci?'

'Different. Bad businessman. Playboy. Is that right word?' Tim nodded. 'Vinci finished.'

'Are they both above law and order?' asked Tim. 'Is *that* how they see themselves?'

'They have their *own* law.'

'Robber barons,' insisted Tim.

'So is British government with taxes!'

They grinned at each other, friendlier now.

'No fight in Sicily, Tim,' said Dino, almost protectively.

'We won't,' Tim assured him. Privately he condemned himself for sounding so feeble, and he still didn't understand where Will stood in all this. Or Dino, come to that. He glanced at his mother and saw that she was reading a Steven King novel while Will knocked back the wine they had ordered. They looked like any couple going on holiday – his stepfather in his Levi's and T-shirt and Mum in chinos and a blue top. No one would ever guess that Will was going to pay back a debt to a Mafia godfather with Mum's money.

As the Boeing descended, Tim could see the ocean nudging against a barren, mountainous landscape which descended to a coastal plain where sun-bleached corn fields and powdery earth gave him an impression of heat and aridity.

The airport was small and its single storey building shone with a blinding whiteness, the glare making the runways and scrubby grass seem watchful, almost threatening. He longed for the softness of England and its misty, concealing dampness. Here there seemed to be no cover at all. Every movement they made would be revealed and exposed.

Tim tried to shrug off his fears as the aircraft landed, but they wouldn't go away, and when he watched his stepfather yawning and stretching he wondered how much he still concealed under this stark spotlight of a sun. Maybe Tim would find out more about him here.

CHAPTER TEN

THE HEAT hit Tim like a blinding wall as they slowly disembarked from the aircraft.

'Don't hurry. I think I might be intercepted here,' Will said casually.

'Intercepted?' asked Marian. 'Who by? One of the godfathers?' She looked round nervously, as if she expected to see one appear from nowhere, walking out of a heat mist, champing on a cigar and wearing dark glasses.

'Keep your voice down, Mum,' hissed Tim, but Will and Dino only laughed.

'They may want to check me out before I see Raphael.'

'Why?' asked Tim.

'See if I'm armed – and if I've really got the money. After all, I might be coming as his enemy – as an assassin.' Will spoke so nonchalantly that he might just as well have been wondering about a choice of hire car. Liar or not, thought Tim, he's certainly cool, and he knew instinctively that his mother must be thinking much the same.

She was. 'You mean these – these men can just turn up where they want to – before we go through immigration and customs or *anywhere*?' Marian sounded aggrieved.

'It's all part of the rich pattern of Sicilian life,' said Will. 'Bribes get you anywhere.'

'Sicily is not the only country where this happens,' snapped Dino defensively.

A man in a customs officer's uniform walked briskly out of the terminal, a clipboard in his hand. He looked very official as he came up to them, while the other passengers filed past, hardly giving him a glance.

'Mr Benson?' He spoke in English.

'Yes?' Will looked wary, as if he wasn't sure of his reception. His laid-back attitude had completely evaporated.

'Please come with me.'

'Sure,' Will said over-casually. 'I shan't be long, Marian. Stay here and I'll be right back.'

But she grabbed his hand, insecure, unable to cope in this sun-blasted place. 'Will—'

'It's OK. I'll be back in a minute. It's only the formality we talked about.' He was irritable now.

'They're not going to keep you—' she whispered helplessly.

Tim intervened before the smiling official stopped smiling. 'He won't be long, Mum.'

Will walked away with his escort and Tim felt

excluded again. Why didn't his stepfather even glance at him? Give him some reassurance?

'Please do not go through immigration control until your husband has rejoined you,' said the young man over his shoulder.

Will tucked the briefcase casually under his arm as if all it contained was a packet of sandwiches instead of £40,000 in high denomination notes. The sun seemed to beat down more intensely, more cruelly.

They hung around in the scanty shade of the airport buildings. Tim looked at his watch. Two o'clock. The Boeing shimmered in the afternoon heat and the refuelling truck seemed curiously out of focus. A flight attendant walked away from the plane, looking like a wraith, and a large pool of iridescent water shone on the horizon. A mirage? He felt exhausted and slightly dizzy. The other passengers had all gone inside the terminal now but the flight attendant didn't query their presence. Perhaps she had seen the young man in the uniform. Or maybe she just didn't care either way.

The Fiat van also looked insubstantial as it drove in their direction, pulling up a few metres away as someone in the back threw out an object which rolled over the tarmac, spilling liquid as it came. Red liquid. Red paint.

The can came to a halt a few centimetres away, leaving a long, sticky stream.

'That's careless,' said Marian vaguely. Then she looked at Tim as the Fiat drove noisily away.

'Careless?' muttered Tim. 'Red paint? That's what—'

Dino muttered something in Sicilian, his face ashen, staring down at the bright, shiny liquid.

The flight attendant paused, wrinkled up her nose. 'What a mess.'

'*So* careless,' Marian repeated, but she was covering up now.

But the woman had noticed Dino's distress.

'Are you all right?'

He stared at her blankly.

'Are you all right?' the flight attendant repeated. 'You look as if you've seen a ghost.' She laughed brightly.

'We have to wait here for my husband,' explained Marian.

The cabin attendant gave her a questioning look. Then she smiled. 'Is he all right?'

'Yes. Someone met him and is having a little chat—' Marian blundered on under Dino's watchful and increasingly uneasy eye. Tim knew what he was thinking. Was Mum going to blow the whole thing wide open?

'VIP treatment, eh?' said the flight attendant.

'That's it,' said Marian vaguely. 'I hope he won't be long. It's hot out here, isn't it?'

The flight attendant nodded and walked briskly

into the terminal while Tim watched the red paint seeping into a drain. Blood for the father. Paint for the son. 'Isn't there a note?' he asked.

'What are you talking about?' Dino protested feebly.

'You *know* what I'm talking about. Why can't you be honest with me?'

Dino shrugged, then said, 'The Don warns him.'

'What about?' demanded Marian.

'There *is* a note.' Dino bent down and picked up the small piece of cardboard that was sellotaped to the tin. He flattened it out and read. 'It means – to regain honour is to be loved again.'

'But he is regaining it,' insisted Marian. 'That's why he's come back.' Tim could see that she was afraid now and that the Mafia was no longer a melodramatic joke.

Will returned a few minutes later, smilingly confident, but when he saw the red paint on the tarmac his expression changed to apprehension. Then he shrugged and the effortless smile returned. He should have been an actor, Tim thought. But he realized that to all intents and purposes that was exactly what his stepfather was.

'Let's go.' Will strode towards the terminal with Dino at his side, showing him the note. Will glanced at it quickly before tearing it into little pieces and scattering them on the ground.

*

The limousine was long, black, highly polished and complete with a chauffeur who at first looked vaguely familiar but who Tim couldn't quite place. Did he remind him of someone in England? Someone at Whispers? Then it came to him. Of course he was familiar. He was Pietro – the old Sicilian who had held Tim at gun point and forced him to help Giuseppe. He was wearing dark glasses, but there was no doubt now about his identity and Tim felt the shock waves pulsing inside him. Pietro showed no sign of recognizing him and Tim looked away quickly, sweat pouring down his face, aware that he had become as much of a conspirator as his stepfather.

'Are we going straight to Don Carlotti's?' asked Marian shakily.

'Yes.' Will seemed subdued now and not at all anxious to talk. The same applied to Dino who was looking at his most sullen.

As Pietro drove the limousine on to an *auto-strada*, Marian seemed to gather more strength. 'We've had the paint before,' she said. 'Is it some kind of warning?'

Will didn't answer the question directly. 'Carlotti will give us round-the-clock protection.'

Marian subsided unwillingly. 'You'd better be right.'

'I am.' Will's voice was reproving, as if he thought she should take his word for it.

'Your track record's poor,' she replied.

For a moment, Tim thought that Will was going to lose his temper and watched him trying to control himself. He only barely succeeded.

Pietro drove the limo towards the mountains, passing a grove of sun-sparkling lemon trees and then a dry river bed. Leaving the *autostrada* they joined a narrow, twisting road that climbed slowly, the narrow bends dropping away into deep, rocky gorges and later into vine and olive-covered slopes.

'Another couple of bends, and we're in Corvo,' said Dino, and Pietro said something in Sicilian.

'What's that?' asked Tim.

'Pietro's saying – he always loves to come back home.'

I bet he does after what happened at Whispers, thought Tim. He wondered how Giuseppe was.

'What do you reckon on Corvo, Will?' asked Tim. He wanted to talk now, to lighten the atmosphere which seemed to be growing increasingly tense. His mother was tapping her fingers on the seat in front of her.

'I was here for twenty years and only left to take yachts up and down the coast. It was a long time – a good bit out of my life. I love Corvo too, but I've always felt a stranger. Despite Carla – and Dino.'

'You haven't mentioned her name for a long time,' said Marian suspiciously.

79

'I don't want to. We spent much of the last five years fighting.'

'And the other fifteen?' she asked.

'They spent those fighting too,' muttered Dino, but he looked as tense and uncomfortable as Marian.

'What about?' asked Tim uncertainly.

'Life,' replied Will. 'We were what you might call incompatible. But now it's over,' he added firmly, dismissing the memory of those years, almost as if he was cancelling them out. 'It's strange coming back like this – as if I'm returning to a life that's over.'

But Tim was sure that nothing was over yet.

CHAPTER ELEVEN

THE VILLAGE of Corvo crouched at the bottom of a long narrow valley, and clustered up the slopes of the mountain. Tim could make out balconies thick with hanging baskets and plants, motor scooters parked in ancient courtyards, alleyways with shrines in the stained walls of the buildings, piles of crates and cartons in a central square, washing stretching across the dark chasms of the streets.

The church began to toll its bell as Pietro drove up towards a small plateau on which stood a stone house in its own grounds surrounded by a high wall. As they drew nearer, Tim could see cameras mounted on it at intervals. The bell seemed an ironic accompaniment to their progress, as if they were on a pilgrimage. But perhaps in a way they were.

Clearly visible, at the end of a track, was what Tim presumed to be Don Carlotti's residence. It was imposing – a square, three-storey white building with grey shutters at the end of a sweeping gravel drive, connected to a series of modern cloisters over which vines trailed. Just outside was a large swimming pool with a fountain at one end and scattered furniture, parasols and a magnificent sculpture of a leaping stallion. There were more outbuildings, and a garage with a white BMW parked outside.

'You'll like Raphael. He's got a kid about your age. Girl called Francesca. Fran for short. He's a widower – his wife was French.' Will volunteered the information as casually as he sprang all his surprises. Maybe he enjoys doing that, thought Tim.

Pietro edged the limo off the road and on to the narrow dusty track with security fencing on either side, winding its way past the olive trees that clung in serried ranks to the rocky, sharply falling ground. Then Tim saw the dark, cloaked shadows running through the scanty shade towards them as the sun glinted on an upraised crucifix.

A group of women dressed in black – about half a dozen of them – blocked their way. One of them held up a gnarled but regal hand, another the tarnished silver cross. Pietro slowed to a halt, dust rising into the early evening sun.

He leant out and began to address them angrily, waving his hand, shooing them as if they were an elderly flock of geese, but the women didn't move.

Then he turned back and shrugged as if they were no longer his responsibility.

'What's up?' asked Marian.

'Nothing,' said Will sharply.

Dino turned away, but the women had already surrounded the car and one of them beat at the window with her fist. She looks like an old lizard, thought Tim. He met her dark angry eyes and was stunned by the loathing in them.

Pietro revved and hooted, but the women stood their ground, shouting one word over and over again in unison. It was a primitive, unsettling chorus.

'What are they saying?' demanded Marian.

'Move!' yelled Will.

'I cannot, sir,' said Pietro, speaking for the first time in English, and seeming to avoid Tim's eye. 'The lady by the front of the car – she is my wife.'

The chanting continued until Will abruptly wound down the window and shouted at them in Sicilian.

But still they stood their ground; black crows, seeking carrion.

Slowly the woman with the cross moved closer to the limo, watching Will with considerable venom, her hatred so intense it seemed to enclose them.

'So the Hawk has returned,' she said in English, her voice full of contempt.

Will tried to laugh, but all that came out was a kind of ludicrous braying sound. Despite the heat, a chill swept over Tim. Something terrible was happening. He reached out for his mother's hand and held it, not sure whether he was trying to give her strength or needing to find some for himself.

'Will – what's going on? You've *got* to tell us,' said Marian.

'Nothing,' rasped Dino. 'Just peasants.' He said something angry in Sicilian.

The woman replied in kind and then broke back into English, 'You the son of the Don – you should know better.'

'*Who*?' gasped Marian.

Dino looked away to the dark mountain summits, now insubstantial in the melting light, no doubt wishing he was amongst them. 'I tell you,' he said, 'they stupid. You should not listen.'

'The Hawk will harm the Don,' said the woman. 'That's why he's returned.'

'No,' Dino at last responded. 'He is here to repay a debt.'

With a squeal of brakes, a Suzuki jeep suddenly careered around the corner in a cloud of dust, with two men in grey suits sitting in the front. The driver got out and came over to the woman, greeting her courteously. He was tall, somewhere in his early fifties, with a long, narrow intelligent face

84

and a diplomatic air, distinguished, polished, eminently reassuring.

'Please – you must go now.' He spoke in Sicilian and then again in English. 'The Don will be grateful for your concern.'

They ignored him, crowding round the car.

'You must go,' he insisted sharply.

'The Hawk – why did you call him that?' Marian turned to the woman, badly shaken, and Will tried haltingly to intervene. He seemed to be as rattled as she was.

'Come on, love. We can't waste any more time.'

'Be quiet,' she said commandingly, returning her gaze to the woman. 'Tell me – why do you call my husband the Hawk?'

The woman didn't reply, but Tim found the compassion in her eyes as she looked at his mother far more terrifying than even the gun battle at Whispers.

'Come,' said the handsome man in the grey suit. 'You must go.'

Slowly, she turned away and began to walk down the track with the other women. They trod slowly between the olive trees, the mellow light absorbing them so that they looked like a dark, shifting cloud.

'I am Luigi Bonstanti – the chief security officer on the estate.' At once, Tim knew that this must be the man Will had spoken to on the phone in the boat-yard office. 'Please do not concern yourselves. There has been an assassination attempt on the Don, that is why the women are afraid, but thank God, he is unharmed.'

Dino looked immediately horrified, but Tim saw that Will was calm.

'Last night his chauffeur drove over a land-mine on the road to Sigosta,' continued Luigi. 'I was behind him. It didn't detonate but the village is tense and suspicious of anybody, everything. More of Mario Vinci's work, most likely. He'd oust the Don if he could.' He turned to Tim and Marian with an uneasy little smile. 'The Don is much loved. He is Corvo's patron.'

'That woman – she said the Don was your father. Not Will?' Marian asked haltingly, as if she was trying to clarify a statement she thought she had probably misheard.

Dino ignored her but Will nodded slowly, almost absently.

'How is that?' she asked blankly.

Tim felt close to tears, unable to cope in this hostile, alien, unpredictable place where even relationships were lies.

Luigi tactfully withdrew as Will began another of his explanations, but Tim knew that he couldn't really believe anything his stepfather said now. Unexpectedly, however, instead of the familiar glibness, Will's words were halting and emotional. Maybe that's another trick though, thought Tim.

'My ex-wife, Carla, had an affair with the Don, and Dino was the result. We brought him up and I cared for him as my own son. I love him – I've always loved him – but he has a special relationship with Raphael too. When Carla and I split up and I decided to leave Sicily, Dino came to England with me. He wanted to travel and the Don was happy he should do this. I'm sorry I didn't tell you the truth.'

Tim waited for the explosion. It wasn't long in coming.

'You're *incapable* of telling the truth,' yelled Marian. 'And why do they think you'll harm the Don? Why were you called the Hawk? How many other lies have you told me?'

Will suddenly put his big handsome head in his hands but Tim knew he wouldn't be allowed to retreat for long.

'*Why?*' persisted Marian.

Tim watched Pietro get out stiffly to offer cigarettes to Luigi and his companion, stretching his old limbs and leaving the argument in the back of the limo to reach its climax.

'I didn't expect this,' Will muttered.

'I bet you didn't,' said Marian with considerable bitterness. 'But you're bloody well going to tell me *everything* now. Everything – do you hear? The *whole* truth.'

'He is called Hawk because he work for my father. He had difficult job,' said Dino, but Tim eyed him suspiciously. Was he simply giving Will breathing space again?

'What were these difficult jobs?' Tim demanded, as angry and purposeful as his mother.

Once again Dino replied as if he were shielding Will from more attack. 'He take men in – and out of Sicily. On boat.'

'Dodgy people?' asked Marian.

'Kind of dodgy,' replied Will at last. He began to speak quickly and he stumbled several times. Because of this, Tim wondered if his stepfather was at last telling them the whole truth. 'I wanted out because I also had to collect money owed to the Don. Bit like being a bailiff. Ironic too – now I'm being pushed to pay back myself. So the Don decided to reward my loyalty and gave me the money to start a restaurant next to the bar. The rest you know.'

'No we don't,' Marian said. 'Why didn't you tell me all this before?'

'Because I wanted to make a fresh start. That's all I ever wanted to do. But the Don called me back.'

'He *had* given you a fresh start,' rapped out

Marian. 'Like I did. We're going to have a lot in common, your Don and me.'

Will was silent.

'So what have you really dropped me and Tim into?' Marian continued.

'I shouldn't have done it, but I couldn't manage without you,' Will said simply, and Tim felt a surge of affection for him. He seemed so alone, and *surely* he must be telling the truth now. 'But there's nothing to be afraid of,' Will added, and Marian gave him a scoffing smile. 'Please believe in me.'

Tim saw Pietro watching them furtively and muttering to his companions. They all seemed chastened. Men might *look* as if they were dominant in Sicily, Tim thought suddenly, but he was sure it was the women who were secretly powerful.

'Why were those women so concerned that Will could bring the Don harm, Dino?' Marian demanded.

'They are just suspicious – after what has happened. There is gossip that Will worked for Mario Vinci. Crazy gossip.'

Woodsmoke rose from the valley below and the cicadas began to sing.

'The rumour was started by Vinci,' Will explained patiently. 'Just to stir it up.'

'You *have* got yourself into a mess, haven't you?' remarked Marian bleakly.

'My whole life's a mess,' replied Will, but Tim

noticed that his pathos was cutting little ice with his mother.

'Do you have anything more to tell us?' she asked menacingly.

'There *is* something else.' Will hesitated, and then spoke in a rush, like an anxious child. 'I was keeping it back as a – as a surprise. We're going to sail back to England in one of the Don's yachts – and we'll be taking Mario Vinci with us. Just for some of the voyage. Now you really *do* know everything.'

There was an incredulous silence.

CHAPTER TWELVE

LUIGI LIT another cigarette and muttered something to Pietro. The Hawk? Tim looked at Will in disbelief. What kind of work *would* he have carried out for Don Carlotti? Did he kill people? The man who had jogged alongside him as they ran by the glistening creek, who had sat down with him to lose himself in another world of books? His stepfather who had rescued him from Torridge – the Hawk? The women from Corvo had made a great impression on Tim. Instead of the peasant stereotypes of a holiday brochure, they had been savagely real, centuries of family loyalty fiercely enshrined in their religious dependence, their true knowledge of good and evil. The soft grey world of England, where lies could so easily be disguised, had fallen away. In this barren place, the truth seemed to flare like a beacon.

'You're taking this gangster. Mario Vinci on a yacht?' Marian laughed almost hysterically. 'With *us*? No way. Think again, Will. Just think again.'

'I have to repay my debt and take a last commission. Those are the Don's wishes,' said Will, making a return to one of his more melodramatic moods.

'You knew he would want this all along?'

'Not all along. No.'

'Why are you taking Vinci?'

'Because he's agreed to leave Corvo. At last.'

'Under pressure?'

'He knows he's bankrupt and has no influence left – no credibility either. The Don is lending him a considerable sum of money to start up a business in France. Of course, it must be repaid.'

'Again? The Don's burnt his fingers with you, hasn't he? I wouldn't have thought he was anxious to set any more people up in business. Unless he's a bit thick,' she added with heavy irony. 'And you say Vinci's been trying to *kill* this Carlotti?' she asked. 'That's rather looking a gift horse in the mouth, isn't it?'

Dino looked at her blankly, not understanding what she meant.

'How much is the fee?' asked Marian bluntly.

'Eighty thousand in sterling. Enough to pay you back – and more.' Will sounded childishly proud of himself.

'What about the money you've got locked away in that account? Why didn't you use that instead of borrowing from Mum?' A long silence followed Tim's confession, but he felt a wave of deep relief.

It was as if he had expelled a demon and no longer had to hold back. But when he looked at Will, he knew he had betrayed him.

'Who told you that?' asked his mother.

'Pietro. Our chauffeur. The guy over there. He was the old man in the Renault. I recognized him immediately,' said Tim.

Marian began to cry. 'I can't take any more of this. There's *always* something else. Always. It's like one of those kaleidoscopes – you look and it keeps changing colour. We look into our lives and they're never what they seem.'

'So you *did* speak to him.' Will was hardly listening to her as he gazed steadily at Tim.

'Yes,' he replied haltingly, for some reason ashamed that he had let his stepfather down. 'I helped Pietro get Giuseppe into the car. He'd been shot, but it was only a flesh wound – like yours. It was as if neither of you really meant to hurt each other. Just to scare – or maybe to warn.'

'Why didn't you tell me all this, Tim?' asked Marian with sudden anger.

'I didn't want to break you both up,' he replied miserably.

'Break us *up*?' She was shattered, not knowing what to say, the tears drying on her cheeks.

Dino and Will waited, as if everyone had reached a crucial point in a game that was far from over. Was that how Will saw it all? wondered Tim.

A game? He looked into his stepfather's face, searching for ruthlessness but now seeing only despair.

'I thought if you found out Will had been lying, you'd leave him and we'd soon be back in Torridge.'

'Let me—' began Will, but Marian wheeled round and told him to shut up. Tim felt her strength of mind but its ferocity made him afraid. Who would win the battle of wits? But he knew the outcome was a foregone conclusion; Will would always have the advantage because he made up the rules as he went along.

'Is this all true?' Already there was a note of defeat in Marian's voice.

'Yes,' replied Will softly.

'And the money?'

'Pietro was lying.' He sounded convincing.

'How can I believe you?' she asked patiently, as if talking to a recalcitrant child. 'Shall I ask him?'

'When we get back to England I can prove it to you, but right now I don't want any more trouble. I'd rather you didn't speak to him,' he pleaded, anxious for a favour.

'How could you drag us out here?' Marian said reproachfully. 'How *could* you treat us like this?'

Does she still love him? wondered Tim, or was this revelation the last straw in their relationship? Had he damned everything by coming clean? Did

Torridge loom? An old grey ghost town where there was no light and no hope.

Will stumbled again as he spoke. 'But you insisted on coming. And I thought if you came there was more chance for us all to share the past – that you would be able to understand me more. I never realized it would all blow up like this. The assassination attempt – those damned ignorant women.'

'I didn't think they were anything of the kind,' said Marian abrasively and there was a long silence. 'When *can* I trust you, Will?' she asked.

He said nothing, staring straight ahead as if he was already facing a judge and jury.

She turned to Tim. 'And you shouldn't have covered up for him either.'

Will took her hand tentatively, knowing he had run the risk of Marian deserting him altogether. 'I want to build up the business – you know damn well I do. This is the past reaching out to me. Once I've done this job – that's it.'

'How *can* I trust you?' she repeated, but Tim could see that his mother was weakening.

'I'll prove myself to you. I've told you that.'

Tim glanced at Dino whose eyes were misted with tears, and he was surprised. He hadn't expected him to be so moved. Maybe the fact that he was Carlotti's son didn't make any difference.

After all, for better or worse, Will and the mysterious Carla had brought him up.

'OK – Will was wrong,' Dino admitted. 'But please – do not destroy him.'

Marian only shrugged impatiently. 'You mean that this man Vinci is going to happily accept exile in France? It doesn't look like it, does it? Not after that land-mine? I would have thought he was still playing his power games.' She turned to Will. 'And you'll be your Don's debt collector now. Will that be another little commission for you – ' she laughed cynically – 'to go and kill Vinci?' Her voice was contemptuous.

'Taking him to France is my last job. I can assure you of that.'

'What sort of trouble will he cause on board this yacht?' Marian's mind switched to the next problem.

'None,' said Will confidently. But it was his confidence that *was* the lie, thought Tim. The ring of confidence that glittered brightly like cheap jewellery.

'I still don't understand.' Marian was speaking less angrily now, trying to find some logic in the convoluted situation. 'If Vinci was going to accept his exile, why should he try to assassinate Carlotti?'

'I'm sure he didn't. It's Vinci's associates who are behind all this, and they may try again. I can imagine how bitter they are at the break-up of his empire – however much of a financial liability it's become. They no longer have influence or power and that's more important than money in Sicily.' Will paused. 'You know everything now. If you want to go home, Pietro will take you both straight back to the airport.'

'No way!' Tim reacted instantly. 'I want to stay and see it though.' He glanced down at the dusty green mass of gnarled olive trees and the thin, rocky soil from which they grew. This wasn't an easy place to live, but the sun was sinking into the mountain in a ball of muted fire, washing the barren slopes crimson. He could hear goat bells and then saw the herd amongst the trees, driven by a boy much younger than he was. Maybe the people did need to be an extended family here with the Don as their godfather. But where did Will fit in? Having been forcibly recalled to pay his debt of honour, he was now being commissioned by one member of the Cosa Nostra to remove another – and receive a large sum for giving him a safe passage. And was that all there was to it? Could the village women be right? Did he present a threat to their beloved Don? And in what way? But the main point of staying, however dangerous, was to find out who Will really was – and what he was made of. 'Please believe me.' The words were so empty, tarnished, but Tim still wanted to believe in his stepfather.

With one last effort, Marian said, 'If there's going to be any kind of future for us, you'll have to be straight with me, Will. Do you understand? Once and for all.'

He nodded acquiescently. Tim was certain he and Mum were peeling back the skins of the onion and there could be many more to come. Right now his stepfather looked humiliated, but Tim wondered if he was playing with them as a kid would. A cunning kid. Tim was reminded of some of the boys from the run-down estate at Torridge. They didn't have much going for them but they were certainly cunning. Will was like them.

Luigi returned, looking uneasy. 'Are you ready?'

'Yes, but could you do me a small favour?' asked Will.

'Of course.'

'Please explain why the women from Corvo call me the Hawk.'

Was Luigi thinking quickly, wondered Tim. Or was he about to make some genuine explanation? It was impossible to tell.

'They mean he used to collect the debts that were owed to the Don. That is all.'

Will turned back to Marian triumphantly.

'I don't know who – or what to believe,' she

replied and ran the back of her hand over her eyes, a gesture she always made when she was tired out and didn't know what to do next. Tim had seen her do this so many times in the past and his heart bled for her. 'Now we're here we'll see it through, but let me tell you this – if you expose Tim to *any* danger, I'll leave you and there won't be any future at Whispers. Not for you, Will.'

'He will take good care of you both – just as he took care of me for many, many years.' Dino spoke with conviction, but Tim could see that his mother was desperate. The kaleidoscope was shifting again.

As Pietro started the engine and Luigi began to back up the jeep, Tim felt a new wave of apprehension. The house loomed fortress-like in front of them, and the high security fence felt sinister and claustrophobic.

As the sun finally disappeared behind the mountain, he could see, beyond the valley, a line of dark blue sea that glimmered in the soft twilight. It looked an inviting escape route.

The track broadened out and became a gravel drive. The house was certainly secure, thought Tim, particularly if this was the only entrance, but what he was not prepared for was the little group that stood in front of the large white building. It was just after seven in the evening now, and in the soft, mellow light he could see a tall man standing with his arms resting on the shoulders of a young girl of about Tim's own age. Don Carlotti was certainly in his sixties, with long silvery hair and a tanned face with a small beard. His white shirt was open at the neck, and he wore dark trousers and polished white shoes. Slim and elegant in jeans and a stylish top, his daughter seemed strikingly beautiful, almost flawless in the romantic Mediterranean light. But as they drew nearer, Tim could see that she had huge eyes with dark shadows under them and a tense, drawn face.

Don Carlotti strode to the limo and flung open the back door. As he did so, a man emerged from the porch and another strolled in from the garden. They stood watchfully, as protective as the women from Còrvo.

'My dear friends, welcome to our home.'

His English is perfect, Tim thought as he and his mother clambered out, feeling awkward and shy. Will and Dino were already kissing Don Carlotti and his daughter, hugging them with such genuine affection that Tim and Marian were overwhelmed. The relationship was deeper, closer than they had imagined.

Releasing Will and Dino at last, Carlotti turned to Tim and Marian, smiling graciously. 'Permit me to introduce myself – Don Raphael Carlotti, and this is my daughter Francesca.' To Tim's dismay there was more embracing and kissing, and the girl smiled at him, as if gently mocking him for his English reserve.

'I would wish you to be happy. Dino and William are familiar with our home, but let me tell his wife and stepson that they are both more than welcome.' Don Carlotti paused as they all moved inside. Then he continued, 'As you can see we have maximum security here. That is because, as a businessman, I have enemies. I am sure Luigi told you of our recent incident. The compound – behind the security fence – is always safe, but if you wish to travel to the beach or the village or up the mountain – you will be accompanied.'

'It's very beautiful—' Marian smiled tentatively at the Don and he gave her a little bow in return – as if asking her to accept them all at face value and no more.

'I hope you will have a pleasant vacation. You are our guests, and we want you to have everything you need. My daughter, Francesca – Fran – will show you round, Tim, and perhaps give you a game of ping-pong while we enjoy some cocktails.'

How patronizing, thought Tim, suddenly aware of the power of this man who could as easily dismiss as welcome him. Maybe he could stamp him out too, like some insect. What was more, he didn't want to spend time alone with Francesca. She seemed as formidable and as potentially dis-

101

missive as her father. Besides, there was the tension in her to contend with as well.

'Am I a grown-up?' asked Dino. 'Or will I be expected to play ping-pong?'

Tim watched the Don's eyes as they rested on his son and saw great warmth in them. He wondered if he would ever see the same expression in Will's when he looked at him.

'You will be expected to drink a large whisky,' the Don warned him.

Dino laughed. 'Thank you – I'll just have a Coke.'

Tim realized that Dino was his own person, that although he rightly expected to be counted as an adult, he had no intention of adopting their ways. Not even the Don's. Tim felt a new respect for him.

CHAPTER THIRTEEN

FRAN WAS silent at first, but after they had played the first game and Tim had accidentally fallen flat on his back whilst trying to produce a spectacular service, she had laughed. Tim didn't mind her laughing at him; she was not derisive or mocking, but there was an edge to her that he found hard to cope with. He wondered as they played on, if Fran knew that Dino was her half-brother. And what was this woman Carla like who had originally been married to Will? Where was she now?

The patio looked down on Corvo and Tim could see scattered lights and dimly hear a transistor radio playing. He imagined the women there and their presence brought him comfort. They might be hostile to Will but he was also instinctively convinced they didn't present a threat to him or his mother. He remembered how the woman in black who had spoken to Will had watched Mum with compassion. Maybe, if the going got rough, they could both run down to Corvo and be cared for.

'We don't eat till late,' said Fran. 'Let's go down to the beach and have a swim.'

'Is it far?' Tim immediately felt uneasy. Had Fran completely forgotten the assassination attempt? Were all their lives in danger now?

Fran must have understood what Tim was thinking for she smiled at him condescendingly, with a measure of her father's easy sense of authority. 'Don't worry,' she said. 'It won't be dangerous.'

'Why not?' asked Tim aggressively.

'We shall have my father's bodyguards. And I can tell you this – no one makes me hide. No one.' She rang a bell on the wall by the side of the pool and Luigi appeared almost immediately, a strange mixture of servant and guardian. 'We want to go for a swim,' she said imperiously.

He nodded. 'I'll bring the jeep.'

'What's it like living like this?' Tim asked.

Fran shrugged. 'It's a habit. Do you have a swimming costume?'

He nodded.

'I'll take you to your room in a minute. Wait here while I get mine. Don't go anywhere,' she commanded.

Tim stood on the terrace, gazing down towards the dark sea. He was beginning to rather like Fran. There was something exciting about her; maybe it was her authority. She made him want to stand up to her, as if she was constantly throwing out a challenge. He wondered what would happen if he did defy her. That could be the exciting part. Tim jumped when he felt a hand on his shoulder. He looked up, startled, into the discerning eyes of the Don.

'I understand that Fran wishes to go for a swim.'

'Is that OK?' asked Tim nervously.

'Of course. She rules me so that her wish is my command. Isn't that an English expression? You will be safe with Luigi and Tonino and you will work up an appetite for dinner.'

Tim was already starving but he didn't like to say so. 'Have you known Will for a long time?' he asked nervously, driven on by an overriding curiosity. But it was *more* than curiosity. Tim wanted to edge nearer to the elusive truth which still seemed to be a speck on a distant horizon.

'Your stepfather has been in my employ for many years and I know all his qualities – *and* his faults. He has much to give, but he can be like a runaway stallion – only harnessed to bolts of lightning which, as you know, are erratic and come from many sources. He wants so much. Too much.'

Tim was surprised at the Don's frankness and he warmed to him at once, flattered that this distinguished man was prepared to confide in him. 'He stole your money,' Tim blurted out more confidently.

'Borrowed,' the Don replied softly. 'He knows

better now. I am sorry about Pietro and Giuseppe. I had not asked for violence, but they were afraid.'

'Of Will?'

'Yes. He is unpredictable.'

'And what about the paint at the airport?'

The Don simply shrugged. 'Paint?' he asked vaguely.

Tim summoned up all his courage. 'Do you trust him?'

There was a long pause. Then Carlotti replied slowly, 'No. But I love him as a brother. It was only after his wife died that he became ruthless.'

'His wife's dead? We didn't know that.' Tim was astounded. But what else could he expect? The revelations seemed endless now, and in his mind's eye he could see them stretching away into infinity.

'She had cancer. It was a great tragedy which affected your stepfather and me deeply. She was a bond between us.'

Tim gazed at the Don, unable really to grasp this latest twist. They were silent for a long time and in the silence he could feel the old man's intelligence and concern, as if they could both see into each other's souls – an extraordinary but comforting sensation.

'Did you not know she was dead?'

'No,' replied Tim.

The Don sighed. 'I'm afraid that William has got used to secrecy. I wish he could be more open

– with all of us. There is something in his nature that resists the truth, but he is still capable of great love.'

'What did this Carla do?' asked Tim.

'She had a vineyard. Carla was the daughter of an aristocrat – a very distinguished, intelligent woman.'

'Why are you telling me all this?' asked Tim. Again he felt proud that this powerful man was talking to him on such an equal level – just as had happened that night when he was with Will and Mum. Tim felt that he had suddenly, unexpectedly, become part of the world of adults – that he was one of them now.

'I want him to have a family again. It was Carla's death that made him so irresponsible. Despite all their quarrels he still relied on her. You and your mother and Dino, you can make him strong again. You can be his healers.'

But could anyone heal a man who lied to himself so much? And for all his warmth and perception, how could Tim trust the Don? Paint for the son, blood for the father. But he was also aware that Don Carlotti had told him he was a healer – and he wanted to heal. *Believe in me*, said his step-father's voice in his mind yet again.

'Before you go,' said the Don. 'I will show you my Sicily. She is beautiful – almost as beautiful as my daughter.'

As he spoke, Fran ran out of the house. 'Where's Luigi?' she asked commandingly. 'He ought to be here with the jeep, and Tim – you must go and collect your swimming costume. Come, I will show you where your room is.'

'There you are.' The Don laughed. 'We are all her slaves.'

Luigi drove fast back down the track and through the shadowed village, the night air warm and smelling of herbs. The constant clicking of the cicadas and the huge pale moon in a starlit sky gave Tim a new feeling of comfort and protection. He and Fran were in the back while Tonino, the other security man, sat in the front with Luigi.

Fran's voice broke into his thoughts abruptly. 'I am afraid for my father. You heard about the landmine? That was terrible. But suppose they try again?' For the first time she sounded vulnerable – as if leaving the fortified mansion had made her unpredictably helpless. The inexplicable excitement inside Tim crept back.

'They won't,' said Luigi confidently, in English. 'We have doubled up the security staff. The danger is over.' He sounded reassuring, and in control, and Tim felt better.

'You know about my father's cousin, Mario Vinci?' Fran said.

'Yes.'

'You are taking him to France. Will has told you?'

Tim nodded.

'How surprising. He usually only reveals things at the last moment.' She laughed. 'Maybe he's learning to trust you.'

'What about your father?' asked Tim. 'Does he trust him?'

'Of course.' Fran replied easily. 'Will used to collect my father's debts. Many people in the village and town of Fortuna had borrowed for business reasons and were unable to pay back. So he sent out William. It did something to him – that job. Then Carla and he split up and later she died and he changed.'

'Changed in what way?' asked Tim.

'He began to work for himself.'

'How do you mean?'

'I mean what I say.' Fran spoke sharply.

'Why are you telling me all this?'

'Because I like you,' she said unexpectedly.

'Did you like Will?' Tim countered, hardly able to cope with all this.

'Yes. But he was not popular outside our house.' Fran paused. 'Then his own debt had to be collected.'

'So you're not pleased to see him back here?'

'I have always found him an interesting man,' said Fran enigmatically.

Then Tim told her about the women from the village and Fran listened, nodding as if the incident had been predictable.

'Debt collectors are never popular. They don't want him here. But my father loves him – like a brother.'

But the Don stole Carla, thought Tim. Could the friendship between the two men really transcend that? Or had they shared Carla and mutually grieved for her? Then another idea occurred to him. Did the Don just take what he wanted? Did Will? Were they both cast in the same mould?

'But you never know what Will feels for anyone,' Fran added.

Tim saw that to explore his stepfather's mind, he would have to take a ball of string, tie it firmly at one end and unravel it through the many secret chambers, blind alleys and distorting mirrors that made up the labyrinth.

'When did Carla die?' he asked.

'Two years ago.' She spoke quickly, dismissively, as if she didn't want to talk about her any more. Perhaps she was regretting confiding in him. Maybe the attempt on her father's life had shaken her so much that she had wanted to talk to someone and now it was no longer necessary. However,

Tim was determined that she would confide in him again and he decided to press her a little harder.

'And Mario Vinci?' he asked. 'What kind of man is he?'

'Weak. And in trouble financially. I believe he's bankrupt.'

'And in debt?'

'To my father? Of course.'

'Is that why he has to go?'

'For his own safety,' replied Fran.

'Is he dangerous?'

'He is manipulative. Like William. My father has been too kind to them both. The trouble is that he still believes in people long after they have proved themselves untrustworthy.' Fran smiled, but her smile was as arid as the darkened landscape. Then she continued, 'William was a stranger here. Even though he had lived in Corvo for so many years and had worked for my father and been married to Carla, it still didn't make him a part of this place. That's another reason the village people didn't like him – the stranger who collected debts. Of course, that made it easier – my father knew that. A stranger has no heart.'

The scramble down to the cove was hazardous. The narrow path wound dangerously near to the edge of the cliff and the air was pungent with herbs as their feet brushed thyme and rosemary on the steep descent.

Finally they reached the small, sandy beach, with Luigi and his companion just behind them.

'You are a strong swimmer, Tim?' Fran asked.

'I'm OK.'

'We'll go to the raft. Do you see it?'

'Yes.' It was out there in the dark, a barely discernible square shape, slowly bobbing up and down in the slight swell.

'You can reach it?' she persisted.

'No problem.'

They stripped down to their swim-suits and plunged in, but not before Tim had taken a quick glance behind him to see Luigi and Tonino, positioned at each end of the beach. They looked reassuringly vigilant.

The water was soft and warm and silky as well as being surprisingly buoyant. Beside him, Fran swam with a swift and powerful crawl, and although Tim tried to match her, she easily outpaced him.

After a while, she stopped and trod water.

'Are you OK?'

'Sure,' he panted. 'You're just faster.'

'I swim every day. You couldn't do that in England?'

'Only if you went to an indoor pool.'

She wrinkled her nose. 'I do not like the sound of that. Is England always grey? I have never been, but William told me this is so.'

'It's often grey. Not always. But you can get homesick for grey amongst the blue.'

'I like you,' Fran repeated as they swam on again, and Tim felt his excitement returning. She was so imperious and athletic that he felt a clod-hopping twit beside her. At the same time, he knew he was beginning to be drawn to her. 'You're not competitive – like most boys. You don't mind being beaten by a girl.'

'I probably do.' Tim tried to be absolutely honest.

'Not in the way most boys do. You're different.'

They were almost at the raft now, heaving in the dark and wave-slapping sea. To one side of the cove there was a group of black rocks around which the waves made an eerie sound; on the other side the headland ran smoothly down to the water.

Tim and Fran hauled themselves up on to the raft and sat down, their legs dangling in the water, looking back towards the beach and Luigi and Tonino.

'It must be great to live here all the year. Where do you go to school?' Tim wanted to have the relief of talking in generalities.

'I go to a convent in Fortuna,' she said briefly. Fran seemed preoccupied, and he waited, hoping she would confide in him again. Eventually Tim's patience was rewarded. 'My father has many prob-lems – it's as if everything is happening too quickly.

He is old now, too old for all this. He has a front – a good front. Is that how you say it in English?'

'Yes.'

'But behind it, he would like the peace we used to have. The safety.'

'Have you always had all these bodyguards? You said you were used to—'

'Never so many,' Fran said impatiently. 'And they didn't come with us when we swam. I often think their presence is an invitation.'

Tim nodded. There was probably something in what she said. 'Why do you think it's got so much worse?' he asked curiously.

'Because my father is powerful, but he's old and his reign is coming to an end. There are many who would like to own his businesses – not only in Sicily but also in America.'

Tim looked up at the cliffs. Some kind of small animal scurried through darkly clustered trees and a large bird flew low over the beach and the bodyguards. The swell increased a little, slapping the sides of the raft, and clouds raced across the face of the moon. He saw that Fran was staring at him curiously, her expression hard to read.

'Is your father religious?' he asked.

'He's Catholic.'

'No – you *know* what I mean.' He found it hard to understand how the Don could sanction so much that was evil.

'He believes in God. He goes to mass—' Suddenly her eyes were full of tears. 'I love my father. He is a *good* man.'

'You don't have to be afraid. The security at the house is so tight and—' He wanted to reassure her, but knew he couldn't. She was too intelligent for that. 'It'll be easier when this Vinci has gone away.'

'Maybe.' She didn't sound convinced.

Tim wondered if he would ever see Fran after they had sailed away, or were these just a few precious moments that he might have to hang on to for the rest of his life?

CHAPTER FOURTEEN

TIM GRABBED Fran's cold wet arm.

'What is it?'

'Someone's up on the headland.' He was sure he had seen something, or was he just over-reacting?

Fran shrugged. 'You're watching shadows.'

Maybe she was right, he thought, feeling stupid. But then his confidence returned. 'Someone was there – I'm sure they were.'

'I shall warn Luigi.' Fran pulled a whistle from around her neck and gave two strong blasts. With a reassuringly fast reaction, Luigi ran forward to the water's edge.

'Let's go,' Fran said, but already Tim could see a speedboat coming round the headland, roaring towards them at full speed, the sound of her engines abruptly cutting into the velvety silence.

'Wait!' he yelled. He couldn't believe this was happening.

'Get in the water. *Now*.' She dived and he followed, catching a glimpse of Luigi and Tonino aiming their guns at their fast-moving target. But they seemed tiny, ineffectual figures a long distance away.

Although Tim had never swum so fast before, Fran was still way ahead of him, but rather than strike out for the shore alone, she turned and waited several times as he struggled to increase his pace.

Then a powerful spotlight shone out from the speedboat and he knew that whoever was behind the wheel intended to run them down.

'Dive.'

Tim felt transfixed as gunfire cracked out from the shore, the echo resounding amongst the rocks, the spotlight blazing into his eyes.

'Dive. Now!' Fran yelled.

She went under and Tim followed, plunging as deep as he could while the speedboat ploughed towards them. The unreality of the situation had disappeared and the panic was as cold and as deadly as the distance he knew he would have to dive.

He opened his eyes under the surface to see Fran's long, thin legs kicking out powerfully below him. Somehow he managed to follow her down, but his lungs already felt as if they were bursting. He could hear the distorted noise of the boat's engine, and when he looked up, Tim could see the propeller above him, its vicious screws turning languidly. So they *had* tried to mow them down;

they had really meant it. But now he had to go up – he couldn't hold his breath any longer – and glancing down he saw Fran looking mermaid-like as she swam below him without any sign of difficulty.

Tim pulled powerfully for the surface and, after what seemed an impossibly long time, broke through to the glorious dark air. The speedboat was heading towards the headland and he breathed in deeply, seeing Luigi desperately signalling to him. But he had to gulp in some air first – wonderful fresh air. As Tim filled his lungs again and again, Fran bobbed up beside him, her dark hair running in silver strands of water. Then he heard the speedboat's engine increase in volume and he turned in numbing horror to see that the craft was returning at an even faster pace, skimming through the waves, the wake behind her stern building into one enormous trough.

They dived again, but Tim was immediately aware that this time he was even weaker. Grimly he knew that he couldn't follow Fran to such safe depths, and if he couldn't make it now what would happen if the speedboat came back time after time?

Once again he looked up to see the propeller screws churning silently above him, and knew he had to come up – and much faster than before.

As he broke the surface for the second time, Tim watched the speedboat departing again – rather as if she was playing with them. He expected her to turn back at any moment but she forged on through the waves, her spotlight beaming ahead, lighting up the scrubby rock face. Then she was gone.

Fran was beside him, gasping slightly but making little noise compared with his own stentorian breathing.

Luigi and Tonino were still on the beach, beckoning to them wildly, shouting loudly in both Sicilian and English.

'Let's go,' she said.

'Who were they?'

'Don't waste your breath.'

On the way back, Tim got a second wind, and soon he was swimming almost as powerfully as Fran. Nevertheless, it still felt like miles to the beach.

But eventually they arrived, forcing themselves to stand, their legs shaking, arms aching, and then running through the shallows towards their would-be protectors.

The chattering sound was above Tim before he realized what it was.

'Helicopter,' Fran cried and he felt as if his legs wouldn't carry him any further. He wanted to lie down somewhere, close his eyes and wait for it all to go away. Luigi ran towards them, yelling, but Tim couldn't make out what he said. His ears seemed to have packed up; it was rather as if he was still under water. The shouted instructions were muffled, incomprehensible, impossible to obey.

'You come,' yelled Luigi. 'You come.'

At last the words became clear as the helicopter flew low over the cliff, continuing on towards Corvo, its chattering sound diminishing.

'Who are they?' Tim shouted at Fran, but she didn't reply as she pulled on her clothes and he clumsily did the same.

Then they were all running towards the steep path. The climb was a panting, frantic run for all four of them, but as Tim stumbled over the loose shale he gasped to Luigi, 'There was a man at the top.'

He nodded, pushing past Fran while Tonino also edged ahead, the barrels of their guns shining in the pale light.

'We go up,' said Luigi. 'I go first – Tonini will stay down just below. You understand?'

Fran nodded impatiently, wanting to move on. Were they after her, wondered Tim. Were they all going to be picked off, one by one?

They waited on the path as Luigi and Tonino spread out in the sparse undergrowth, creeping up through the trees, crouching down, waiting, and then moving on again. A great stillness descended on them, and when Tim looked down he had the eerie sensation that the sea was no longer making any noise and had become completely motionless, like a painted ocean. A lizard ran over his hand, its contact dry and feathery. The creature stopped to look at him, eyeing him curiously and then scuttling away.

Luigi ran back down the path. 'I can't see anyone, but that doesn't mean anything. You run with me and then get into the jeep. OK?'

Tim was reminded of jogging with Will as they all pounded up the shale in single file behind Luigi who still had the gun ready. Then his nerves screamed as Tonino shouted something in Sicilian and Luigi hissed, 'Get down behind me. Get down now.'

As they flung themselves to the rocky ground, Tim could again smell the pungent scent of rosemary that was now so associated with danger. Why had Will ever allowed them to come to this place, he thought unfairly, illogically. Mum was right; he didn't care about anyone but himself.

They seemed to lie on the sharply rising ground for a very long time and Tim could feel the heat of the past day permeating him. He could just see Luigi's dusty shoes and, behind him, he could hear Fran breathing.

There was a muttered word from above and Luigi whispered, 'It is OK.'

'What was it?'

'A dog.' The black dog of the past, wondered Tim wildly.

Fran sniggered and he had the mental image of Tonino chasing the animal. A great wave of relaxation swept through him and he longed to give vent to explosive giggles – and probably tears – and he suspected Fran felt exactly the same.

'Move!'

They reached the clifftop gasping and panting, Luigi and Tonino surprising Tim by their sudden athleticism. Earlier they had stumbled down to the beach; now they were running like gazelles.

Then he caught sight of the jeep. Even in the pale moonlight he could see the bonnet was splashed with a dark substance – a substance he instinctively knew was red paint.

They stood in front of the vehicle while Luigi swore quietly.

'They're going to kill him – kill my father tonight. *That's* what the helicopter was for – that's where it was heading.' Fran was rapidly losing control.

'The house is secure,' Luigi said reassuringly. 'There *is* no problem.'

But Fran, forgetting any kind of caution, began to yell at him, 'We've got to get back. Don't you understand? We've got to get back.' Her fear was contagious.

Luigi cried out sharply, 'Wait!' for she was running towards the jeep. 'Let me check it out. It could be booby-trapped.'

They paused, Fran shaking, while Luigi cautiously lay on the ground and pulled himself under the chassis and Tonino leant over the driver's seat, examining the ignition, feeling gently under the dashboard and scrutinizing the handbrake. While the inspection continued, Tim put his arm round Fran's shoulders.

'It'll be all right,' he said.

'Don't be a fool,' she snapped back, pulling away from him. 'You know nothing.'

Eventually, Luigi and Tonino were satisfied that there was no booby trap, but the return drive was terrifying as Luigi steered round blind, steep bends, the engine roaring and revving, dust and chips of rock rising in the air behind the rear wheels in a dense cloud. The vehicle swayed alarmingly as the road became steeper, and Tim wondered what would happen if they met a car or a truck round the next corner. The valley below was lit by bleak moonlight and he could see the pale course of the dried-out river bed. Spiky foliage clung to its arid banks and, further along, there was the upside-down wreck of a small, burnt-out van.

Beside him Fran was weeping.

'They'll kill him. The men. The men in the helicopter. They've come to kill him.' She was beside herself with fear and anger and terrible frustration.

'Please, God, help him,' Fran began to repeat over and over again. 'Please, God, help him.'

It was impossible to reassure her as the jeep bucketed, roared and screamed its way up the mountain, so Tim put his arm round her again, holding her rigid body as close as he could. This time she didn't shrug him away.

The journey back to the house seemed incredibly long, and Tim kept thinking he could hear the chattering of the helicopter above the jeep's gunned engine.

Suddenly there was a dull thud and an almost immediate explosion, like an elongated clap of thunder that went on and on, growing in strength and fury. Luigi swore, but Fran stopped crying and pushed Tim away, her eyes fixed ahead.

'What's happening?'

'The helicopter – it's come down,' she said.

'Maybe a bomb,' yelled Luigi.

At once Fran began to rock herself to and fro and Tim knew better than to try and touch her now. He thought of his mother – and Will – and the panic hit him like a punch in the stomach, and, in his imagination, he already saw the Carlotti house as an inferno.

As Luigi skidded the jeep around the final bend, Fran yelled, 'It's in the field. Outside the fence.'

The bright red flames were clearly visible now, accompanied by a surging pall of dense black smoke which was blowing in a light wind towards the sea.

Tim could see the white BMW entirely blocking the track, and Luigi slammed on the brakes, just avoiding a collision. For a minute the silence was punctuated only by the crackling of the fire, but soon there was another dull thud and a blinding white light, followed by thicker smoke.

'That's the helicopter's fuel tank,' said Luigi more calmly. 'Tonino, you stay back with the kids.' He spoke in English, admonishing them. 'You not come. Right?'

They both nodded miserably as he began to run towards the house. They waited, listening, picking up what Tim thought was the sound of gunshots. Meanwhile the helicopter continued to blaze behind the security fence, the smell of burning fuel almost overcoming them, as Tonino turned to right and left, his finger on the trigger of his automatic.

'Can't we see what's happening?' asked Tim, but Tonino ignored him. 'Can't we—'

Fran intervened, trying to calm herself but failing. 'He doesn't speak as much English as Luigi.'

'Tell him to let us go in.'

'I can't, Tim. We have to obey security – whatever happens. My father told me always to do that.'

The long drawn-out silence continued until he was conscious once more of the sound of cicadas underneath the crackling of the flames. Then a familiar voice rang out of the darkness.

'It's me. William. I've got my wife, Dino, and Mario Vinci. We need the jeep. There may be survivors from the chopper – and they could be armed—'

'Vinci?' Tonino tried to understand and clearly failed. 'Why you have Vinci?'

'He came up by car about ten minutes ago to warn us that his associates had planned another attack. We were terrified for Tim and Fran, but there was no time—'

'I don't understand,' said Tonino. 'You stay there or I shoot.'

'I understand.' Fran was in control again, her collapse forgotten and she spoke to Tonino quietly and with considerable authority in Sicilian.

'Because of Vinci's warning we were ready for them, thank God.' Will sounded more flurried now. 'The security people here knocked out the chopper but we've got to leave. Right away.'

Again, Fran translated what Will was saying to Tonino and Tim listened, dazed by the traumatic turn of events. His stepfather seemed in charge now, but where was Don Carlotti?

'Where is my father?' asked Fran in anguish, voicing his thought.

Where was *Will*? wondered Tim. Somewhere

round the back of the BMW? He couldn't see anyone.

There was a fractional hesitation before his step-father replied. 'He's in the limo.'

'Is he hurt?'

'He's in the limo,' Will repeated as he came into view, wrenching open the door of the BMW. 'I'm going to back this up. Get it out of the way. We'll all use the jeep.' He looked mesmerized, almost as if he was thinking about something else.

Tonino nodded agreement but Fran croaked, her voice hoarse with anxiety and her English confused in an agony of despair, 'Did you hear me not? My *father* – is he hurt?'

'He's injured,' said Will reluctantly. 'He was on the terrace as the chopper came over and they got a shot at him. Pietro and Sebastian – they're going to take him to the hospital in Fortuna in the limo, but we have got to get Vinci out immediately. The longer he stays round here, the more trouble there's going to be. That helicopter may have a lot of back-up, so let's move!'

Tonino put the jeep into reverse while Will got into the BMW with Dino. Suddenly the limo careered round the bend from the house, its lights flashing and horn blaring. As it ground to a halt, in its headlights Tim saw his mother at the side of the track, looking dazed, while beside her a small fat man was being sick on the wiry grass. Tim guessed that this must be Mario Vinci. There was a cut on his forehead and his round, almost innocent-looking face was haggard. A few metres away the helicopter was still burning vigorously, the black pall of smoke a ragged blemish on the pale night sky.

'You OK, Mum?' yelled Tim.

She nodded and he knew that she couldn't trust herself to speak. With screaming tyres the other vehicles reversed up the track while the limo inched forward. Once they were back on the road, Tonino turned the jeep round fast and waited while Mario Vinci and Marian ran towards them, followed by Will and Dino. Meanwhile, the limousine, still with its lights flashing, drove off at considerable speed and the others clambered into the jeep behind Tonino.

'We're going to the harbour,' said Will.

'I can't leave my father,' wept Fran. 'He is dying.'

'He's not.' Will was more commanding than Tim had ever seen him.

'I'm getting out.' Fran struggled towards the door but Will grabbed her. 'Your father said you were to come with me,' he shouted furiously. 'You must do what he says.'

'Why?' yelled Fran.

'Because he's your father.'

'I want to go back to him.' She struggled harder but Will held her fast.

Could Vinci really be a Mafia boss? Tim wondered. He looked more like a bank manager. But maybe it was Mario Vinci's unmarked baby face and lack of stature that made him so sinister. So he had warned the Don that his enemies – Vinci's associates – were on their way. Why had he done this? Had he really accepted his exile, Tim wondered, or did he have some other agenda? If so, what could it be?

Fran kicked hard at Will and then again, but he still held on to her with considerable strength. 'They'll kill you,' he said. 'They were even going to kill Mario for running out on them. Without a leader, they're just a pack of disorganized thugs, but they're still lethal.'

Fran subsided as the jeep roared and rattled back down the coast road, taking the bends at the same horrifying speed. She sat limply, looking down at the floor and putting up no further resistance. Meanwhile, the limo had been lost to sight.

'It won't be long, Mum,' said Tim hopefully, but she was silent, shaking, trying to keep her eyes away from the abyss below.

Will tried to comfort Fran. 'The Don will be all right. You *must* believe me.'

'Believe you?' she said. 'No one in their right mind would *ever* believe you.'

For once his stepfather had no answer; to Tim's surprise he turned to Marian as if Fran had hit him. Then he saw his mother squeeze Will's hand and he suddenly felt more hopeful and optimistic. In theory she ought to be agreeing with Fran, but he realized that once again, as he was often forced to do, she had gone back to the baseline. Despite all Will had done and all that had happened in the few hours since they had arrived in Sicily, she still loved him.

'Listen, Fran,' Vinci interceded with surprising authority, speaking in good, careful English. 'They tried to kill your father – they could try to kill you. You're safer on the yacht and you can telephone the hospital from there.'

'They have already tried to kill Francesca and the boy,' said Tonino, gripping the bucking wheel and steering with maximum concentration. Nevertheless, as he drove, he managed to explain what had happened in the cove, and when he had finished, there was a long silence.

'Where's Luigi?' asked Tonino.

'He's OK. He said he would bring the Saab and meet us down at the harbour. The rest of the security staff can cope with any survivors from the chopper,' said Will quickly. 'God, what a mess.'

'My colleagues have much to lose by my departure,' said Mario Vinci. 'Their family has lost its father.'

But Tim was no longer listening for he had noticed the blood dripping from the sleeve of Dino's shirt.

'You've been shot—'

'No – I cut my arm on some broken glass when I dived for cover on the terrace. Trouble is – the blood will not stop coming. Look – ' he began to laugh, 'it's just like the paint.'

Dino's laugh continued, peal after peal, until Will reached across and slapped him round the face. 'I'll put a tourniquet on for you,' he said. He pulled off his own T-shirt and began to rip it into an improvized bandage. As he worked on Dino in the swaying rear of the jeep, Will tried again to reassure Fran. 'I was with your father when he was shot. The bullets entered his shoulder and his left side – just above the ribcage. Both passed through cleanly – and I *do* know what I'm talking about. Try and trust me. I know it's difficult, but they're both clean wounds and he's going to live. OK?'

Fran nodded, the tears continuing to roll down her cheeks, and Will put his arm round her. She didn't resist. Tim felt a twinge of jealousy for he would have liked to have done that himself. There she was, snuggling up to a man she didn't trust. But then they had all done that – in their own way.

CHAPTER FIFTEEN

TONINO WAS driving on the coastal plain now, and released from the tension of the bends Tim tried to be objective. He knew he needed to be calmer, try to think ahead, but all he could do was to review the bizarre plight they were in. Only a year ago, he and Mum had been living in Torridge. Now they were squeezed into the back of a jeep with a Mafia boss, a godfather's daughter, and a godfather's illegitimate son. He glanced at his mother and was suddenly amazed. She was no longer outraged, indignant and afraid. Instead, she looked in charge of herself, like one of those gangster's molls that he had seen in old black and white films on TV on Sunday afternoons. Then the jeep hit a rut and he heard his mother ask Will, 'If those people – Vinci's people – can attack the house, won't they attack the boat?' Her voice was curiously matter-of-fact.

'Tonino's going to do a decoy job with the other yacht. We've got it worked out.'

'But what about helicopters?'

'There is only one,' replied Vinci. 'And that was my own personal aircraft – the one that is burning in that field,' he added bitterly. 'My associates wanted to kill the Don and his staff, burn the house – wipe out everything that was his. Then they thought I would return to my old position of power. But how could I? I still owe much money and killing the Don would not help. How could it? They acted blindly, stupidly.'

'What about the speedboat that tried to run us down when we were swimming?' asked Tim suspiciously.

'That was mine too. There is no doubt that it is time for me to leave this country – I am bankrupt and can no longer control my employees. Besides, I accept my exile, my new beginning. The Don has been good to me and I will try and repay him.'

Tim still couldn't understand why this man had accepted being bailed out by an enemy. Nor could he understand why the Don should have bailed out Mario Vinci in the first place. Surely he would be better dead. Or was Will to be his assassin? The sudden thought shocked him deeply.

Fran had shut her eyes against it all, her knuckles white as she gripped the seat in front of her. Will's arm still rested around her shoulders. Who should I tell, wondered Tim desperately. Who would accept that Will might be Vinci's assassin? His final job for the Don. Then he wondered why it should be final. Perhaps it was just *another* job for the Don.

The jeep passed the headland where a few hours earlier they had run down the path to the beach. It seemed far away in the distant past. What was more, after all they had been through together, Tim felt as if he had known Fran for most of his life, yet he had only played a game of ping-pong and taken a swim with her before nearly being rammed by a speedboat. But they had talked. They had really talked.

Suddenly lights swamped the jeep's interior and Mario Vinci shouted, 'Someone's on our tail.'

Tim saw Tonino stiffen, but Will replied calmly, 'That'll be Luigi in the Saab. Stop worrying! It's going to be all right now.'

Tim saw that Fran was still crying, silently now. 'Will's right,' he tried to reassure her. 'The danger's over.'

'Right? Him?' She was speechless with fury as she jerked away from Will's arm. 'You don't know what you're talking about – so just keep quiet.' Tim could feel the real force of her anger now.

'Why not break it up, you two?' Marian shouted above the noise of the engine.

Tim saw the sweep of the bay and the harbour wall behind which yachts clustered around neat jetties, with their wooden slats and mooring posts. Bright security lights sharply illuminated varnished wood, well scrubbed decks and polished metal rails. The marina was peaceful, well ordered and silent except for the chink of rigging and the quiet lapping of the tide. Outside the dark sea surged lazily against the harbour wall. Tim looked at his watch. Two a.m. They had been in Sicily since seven. During those few hours there had been an attack from a speedboat and then a helicopter. This was the stuff of James Bond, of Indiana Jones, yet it was all real and Tim had never been so petrified with fear in his life. Whispers, the creek and the marshes all seemed hundreds of thousands of miles away. Light years – another planet.

The jeep, followed now by the Saab, pulled up outside the security gate, the engine ticking over so loudly that Tim thought they must be announcing their presence to every potential assassin in Sicily. Then Tonino switched it off and the swamping silence was much, much worse.

'When I go – you follow,' said Will crisply. 'And move. Luigi will come with us and Tonino will take the *Celeste*. We'll be going in the *Marie*. And yes – I know the names are ironic, but that's the Don's sense of humour. Directly we're on board I want everybody else to go below. I'll be in the wheel-house and Luigi will keep watch. OK?'

They all nodded dutifully and Tim wondered how his stepfather could make jokes at a time like this after all that had happened. Was this terror just a game to him? The kind of game chameleons were good at? Surely after all their efforts, Vinci's men weren't going to give up now, but there was no sign of any headlights on the mountain road.

Nevertheless, Will and Tonino were out of the jeep immediately, ducking under the barrier, Tonino streaking out in front. Tim leapt down, turning to see if he could help his mother, but to his surprise she was already ahead of him, running like a young girl and almost pacing Will. He had the feeling that she would have overtaken him if only she knew where the *Marie* was. Tim ran to catch up with her, panting. Behind him Vinci and Fran ran incongruously together, while Dino, wincing, brought up the rear with Luigi.

Tim's heart lightened as he watched his mother leap over a rope. He was so proud of her, seeing her perhaps for the first time as a woman and not just a mother – someone who was not shackled to a home and responsibility. Had it taken a Mafia vendetta to bring that about? He thought of the Don, hopefully now having the medical treatment that would save his life. It would be terrible if the old man died, for whoever he was, whatever he had done, Tim had been drawn to the power of his personality – and to his obvious love for Will. Then his thoughts turned yet again to Fran. He would do anything for her. Romantic fantasies of heroic deeds filled his mind as he ran along the

136

quayside. He saw himself rescuing her from the sea, from the Mafia, from pirates, from an endless line of enemies, real and imaginary.

Then Tim went flying over a winch and landed on his back, winded and gasping for breath. When he looked up, Fran was bending over him, offering her hand, but there was no mockery in her eyes, only concern. Tim remembered what she had said when they had been swimming. *I like you. You're not like other boys.*

'Are you hurt?'

He struggled to his feet, his hand in hers, discovering her strength as she pulled him up.

They ran on together and Tim's spirits rose. He forgot the shock of death and destruction and only saw friendship. The dowdy dragon of Torridge was vanquished forever.

CHAPTER SIXTEEN

THE *MARIE* was large, well equipped and ready to put to sea. At the next jetty, her sister yacht, the *Celeste*, was already motoring out of the marina with Tonino at the helm.

As they boarded the carpeted gangway, Tim wondered again about Mario Vinci's fate. Why had he warned the Don about the attack? Was he really accepting his exile so philosophically? Why had the Don loaned him money to start up again in another country? Wouldn't he simply become a threat again? Was Vinci in some way in league with Carlotti? With Will even? Or was he simply going to be disposed of once they were at sea? The questions pounded in Tim's mind, producing a blinding headache and isolating him even from his own mother.

Below decks, the accommodation was luxurious but Tim was not soothed by the civilized atmosphere. He could remember all too well the frenzy he had felt when the speedboat had attacked him and Fran. The sheer terror of being forced to dive down to those impossible depths, and the chaotic and panicky escape in the jeep down the mountain road had made him so tense that he knew sleep would be impossible. The warmth and security of the *Marie*, the quiet humming of her generators, the deep pile carpet, the huge white sofa and chairs, the polished central dining table with its scattered, exotic Mediterranean flowers and the clinking of the chandelier above him merely seemed to present yet another threat.

'Get some sleep if you can – we're going to be at sea for quite a time,' said Will quietly.

Dino collapsed on to one of the sofas, but the others sat round the table and listened in relieved silence to the throbbing of engines and the sounds of Will and Luigi casting off ropes and bringing up the anchor. Tim wondered how they could be so placid after all that had happened.

Will walked across to the ship's telephone and began to dial. 'I know he's going to be all right,' he said, but Fran's despair immediately resurfaced and she turned away, muttering in Sicilian. But Will was already talking rapidly and then listening carefully, nodding occasionally. When he put the receiver down and turned back to the table, Tim saw that some of his buoyancy had disappeared.

'He's dead, isn't he?' Fran's voice was horribly controlled, completely expressionless, and she was staring now at Mario Vinci as if she would like to kill him herself – here and now with her bare hands.

'He's in intensive care. We must pray for him,' said Will.

'Are they hopeful?' asked Dino fearfully.

'Of course,' said Vinci scornfully. 'He is a great warrior.'

Fran closed her eyes and Marian put her arms around the girl; a long, uneasy silence began to develop. It was as if they were praying for the life of a king, Tim thought.

Will phoned the wheel-house, spoke again in rapid Sicilian, and then told everyone that the yacht was on auto-pilot. 'I'm not heading out to sea tonight though,' he said authoritatively. 'We'd be too much of a target in the dawn, so we're going to anchor at Lanatia cove – near the coast-guard station. There's a busy shipping lane nearby and I want to be right in the centre of it tomorrow. They're less likely to attack us if there are plenty of other vessels around. There are separate cabins for everyone,' he continued. 'I suggest you kids and Mario take one each. Marian and I will share and Luigi is already on watch. He'll wake me about four and I'll take over.'

'Have you been on the *Marie* before?' asked Tim curiously.

'I've taken her up and down the coast – and much further – dozens of times.'

'Let's all turn in,' proposed Marian, running a gentle, soothing hand down Fran's cheek. 'Would you like to come with me tonight, love? Will can have a single cabin.'

Tim saw the look of mistrust on his stepfather's face. Then it abruptly disappeared and he spoke briskly. 'I'll try the hospital again when I change the lookout shift with Luigi. I'll wake you and give you the news.'

'If you remember.' Fran's voice was cold.

'I'll remember.'

Will showed Tim to his cabin, which was equipped with TV and video, a soft white carpet and a real bed screwed to the deck rather than a bunk – a bed that looked so comfortable that Tim felt the tension draining away and could suddenly think of nothing else but sleep. He sank down on its soft downy duvet.

'Let me ask you something.' Will sat awkwardly on the side of the bed.

'Mm?'

'I wouldn't have put you and Marian through this for anything, you know that, don't you?'

'Sleep,' Tim muttered. 'Must sleep now.'

'I know.' Will patted his shoulder. 'But give me another few seconds.'

'What is it?' Tim turned over with considerable effort, gazing up into his stepfather's tanned face. What *was* his expression? Concern? No – more

than concern. Anxiety? A desire to convince? A
need to – Tim's judgment petered out at this point
as the welcome exhaustion attacked him again. He
could hide in sleep – blot everything else out.

'Do you trust me with your mother?'

'You know I do,' said Tim wearily.

Will was silent. Then he said, 'You can trust me
too. I'll never let you down. Now get your sleep.'
He leant over and kissed him on the forehead. 'Try
and forgive me. The past is over.'

Tim felt the little flame of hope spread inside
him again. 'You weren't to know they'd attack the
Don,' he said generously.

'No.'

'Then stop punishing yourself.'

'It's hard. I had no idea Vinci's people would
do this. I thought they'd accepted his empire had
collapsed. Now the Don could die and there's Fran
– she adores him.' Then Will abruptly changed
tack. 'We'll be back in England soon and I'll start
work on Whispers again. It'll all be different.' Tim
wanted so much to believe him and go to sleep,
but Carla's name surfaced in his mind and he knew
he had to raise her ghost. Was she really the reason
why Will had become so devious?

'The Don told me your – Carla died from
cancer.'

'That's right.'

He plunged on. 'Have you ever got over that

Will? I know Dino said you were always arguing, but—' Tim broke off, not liking to add that the Don had confided in him that Carla had been important to them both.

Will remained inscrutable. 'Yes.'

'You sure?' he persisted.

'I have you and Dino and your mother. You're all I want.' There was a note of absolute sincerity in his voice, and Tim felt the affection he had for Will return.

'Do you think the Mafia will ever lose power?' he said to cover the relief that was spreading through him.

'The Cosa Nostra is crumbling already. The trade unions and the students and the farmers' co-operatives have been demonstrating against them. That never used to happen. They chant, *Pace si, Mafia no! Pace si, Mafia no!*'

'But you worked for them for years,' protested Tim, now desperately wanting Will to confide in him. All thoughts of sleep had completely disappeared. 'Let's face it, you were one of them.'

'Sure. I was a cheap little crook. I'm not like that any more, but I've still got a lot of respect for the Don. One part of him is ruthless – the other compassionate. He supports all kinds of charitable causes and then there's Corvo—' He sounded almost propagandist.

'You were his debt collector,' Tim reminded him.

'I know. It didn't make me popular, but the Don's dealings with the village were not dishonourable – unlike most of the godfathers. But I'd like to see them all go – and they will soon because public opinion is so much against them.' He paused, adding passionately, 'The students in Palermo published a poster with a poem on it by Brecht. I've learnt it by heart. Want to hear it?'

'Is it good?' Tim felt that somehow he was colluding, borne along by a flood tide. He remembered how he had imagined the water in the creek emptying out towards Sicily.

'As powerful as anything Dickens wrote.' Will began to recite softly:

'The great oak,
the glory of the emperor,
is falling:
and who would ever have said so?
It was not the river, not the storm
that split the great trunk to the roots, but
the ants, thousands of ants,
working every day together,
organized, for years and years.
Soon you will listen to its fall
and the tremendous crash, and an immense cloud of dust
will rise after the fall.
And the little plants of the world
will finally see the sun.

The little people – that's whose side I'm on,' Will assured him.

'What about us? Mum and me? Do you really love us as much as you loved Carla?'

'Yes.' Again Will sounded totally convinced and Tim hoped he could see love in Will's eyes. 'Although we'd already parted, Carla's death nearly did for me, and when I met your mother I knew that God had given me back the happiness and the joy that had been taken away. It was like a miracle. It's *still* a miracle. You and your mother and Dino – you're more precious to me than anyone in this world. God bless you.' His stepfather's voice broke and Tim was moved in spite of all his suspicions. But it was a familiar enough pattern. Yet again he felt the confliction of his emotions: he loved Will – and he was suspicious of him. The two feelings now ran parallel.

Tim reached out for Will's hand. 'I care about you, Will, and I trust you.' He had to be positive, to make an affirmation.

'Same goes for me,' he replied.

Tim was going to say more, but the desire to sleep had abruptly returned and he rolled on to his side, put his head on the pillow and closed his eyes. He had a last fleeting vision of Will smiling down before Tim drifted into comforting oblivion.

*

But his oblivion was to be transitory and he woke to a knocking at the door.

'Come in,' he said, expecting his stepfather. Instead it was Fran, looking exhausted in grubby T-shirt and jeans, her hair rumpled. Even now she was running a hand through it. But Tim thought he had never seen a girl look so beautiful.

'Can I come in?'

'Sure.'

'I can't sleep, and your mother and stepfather are talking.'

'What about?'

'She doesn't trust him.'

Tim sighed. 'What's new?'

She rather hesitantly placed herself on the bed where Will had sat. 'I was right to be afraid for my father. I know he will die.'

'No one else seems to think so.' Tim fought against his fatigue. He wanted to reassure her, but it was so difficult. 'Will says the Don's too tough for that,' he added.

'He's wrong. No one knows him as I do. He's old and weak and this Vinci business has cost him so much in energy. The money doesn't count. He took a risk in trying to break up his organization.'

'And you don't trust Will?'

'How can anybody?' she asked.

'I try.'

'I can see why you do – and why your mother

does too.' Fran was surprisingly understanding. 'He's capable of love.' She sounded as if she was making a big concession. 'He loves my father. But William is a survivor and he *has* to put himself first. If he doesn't, he'll fall into a thousand pieces. Like your nursery rhyme – *Humpty Dumpty*. And no one could ever put him together again. William invented himself. Do you know what I mean?'

'I think so.'

'Somewhere, in some distant place, there is the real him.'

But as Tim was wondering whether that distant place could ever be Whispers, the cabin door burst open and his stepfather stood on the threshold. He looked more angry than Tim had ever seen him before, and he guessed that Will was wondering if they had been talking about him.

'Come on, Fran – you *must* get some sleep. And Tim's worn out.'

As she left, she said, 'God bless you, Tim.'

This time, he didn't plunge into oblivion so easily.

Eventually, however, Tim slept deeply and woke slowly, at first not knowing where he was. He had dreamt that he and his stepfather were running alongside the creek, pursed by the women from Corvo. Then he saw that the Don's limousine was cruising slowly in the opposite direction with Tonino at the wheel and the windows open. The Don leant out, holding a can of Walpamur Vermilion. Slowly the limo overtook them, and as it did so he threw the paint over Will who fell back into the arms of the woman with the crucifix.

As the nightmare faded, the gentle rocking motion of the *Marie* reminded him of where he was and Tim glanced at his watch. Just before nine. It would be great to go and have a swim, especially if Fran was awake. He put on shorts and a T-shirt and opened the cabin door.

The state room was deserted, looking fresh and pristine as if no one had ever been there. The deck was empty as well, but Tim guessed that the others were still asleep in their cabins, and although he supposed Will must be in the wheel-house, he was immediately distracted. There was no wind, hardly any swell and the sea was a glassy blue. It looked so inviting that he longed to dive straight in.

Leaning over the side he saw that they were anchored in a small sandy cove which was dominated by tall, tree-clad cliffs that soared ruggedly to a small house. For a moment he saw a flash of light from one of the open windows and wondered if someone was watching him through binoculars. Surely he ought to go and tell Will, particularly after all that had happened. But the water was having a hypnotic effect on him and Tim had to plunge in. Nothing else was important.

The sea was as wonderful as he had thought it might be – warm, silky, but with a cool edge that was enormously refreshing. Tim struck out for the beach, cleaving the water in a fast crawl, smelling brine and seaweed and purity. Yes, he thought, purity did have a smell, but it was hard to put into words. The phrase 'alpine fresh' came into his mind and he laughed. Brainwashed by commercials, he thought inanely.

He swam on towards the beach, a heady feeling of physical well-being overcoming him. He remembered what Fran had said: 'God bless you.' Maybe they would be friends for life, however much she disliked Will. He had so many mixed feelings about her but the overriding one was joy. And maybe she was right – that he would find his stepfather's real self in some distant place. Once in the shallows, he got up and ran on to the warm sand. The sun was climbing high in the sky, brushing his shoulders with the promise of its heat, and he felt so elated that he turned a couple of cartwheels. Then Tim's thoughts once again returned to Fran.

He had never had a girlfriend before, had never wanted one, but this experience was different. He sat down on the sand, running its fine grains through his hands, steeped in optimism and longing. If only Will and Mum could be happy too;

maybe she would forgive him, once all this was over. He remembered Will's words last night. 'You and your mother and Dino – you're more precious to me than anyone in this world.' Surely everything was going to be all right now. They had suffered enough.

Tim ran back into the shallows, waded out and turned over on his back, lazily kicking his legs. After a while he turned again and swam back to the yacht. Soon he must go and find Will, wake them all up. Unwilling to leave the water yet, however, Tim began to swim around the yacht with a slow breast-stroke.

As he rounded the stern, he saw the body floating face down, one foot entangled in the anchor chain. It was as if a silent scream howled through his soul. The horror was beginning all over again.

CHAPTER SEVENTEEN

TIM STARED numbly at the thing. It was wearing a striped shirt and slacks and the hair was short, the head round, the body fat. One arm was underwater, the other stretched out, the fingers floating on the surface as if they had a life of their own. Mario Vinci.

Tim felt unable to move, eternally treading water, gazing hypnotically at Vinci's corpse, his mind a blank, the numbness spreading. At length, spluttering with fear, he forced himself to make short, sharp little swimming strokes back to the ladder at the stern of the *Marie*. Will. Mum. Fran. Dino – where were they? He began to call out their names but only swallowed water and ludicrously spluttered even harder. Soon he was clambering up the ladder, breathing in little gasps, running to look in the empty wheel-house and then pounding over the deck and down the companion-way ladder to Will's cabin. He thundered on the door and rattled the handle, but there was no reply and the door was locked.

Tim ran feverishly to the cabin his mother and Fran were sharing and saw that the door was slightly open. It was empty; there were no signs of a struggle but the sheets were pulled back. He ran on, but they were all in the same condition; the sheets neatly drawn aside as if they had all responded to a calm and unthreatening knock at the door. The *Marie Celeste*! In spite of his panic, Tim momentarily registered the new irony of the Don's choice of names.

Racing back to his mother's cabin he began to search, discovering that her clothes had gone and so had her walking shoes. There was no watch – and no sign of the little green bead necklace she always wore.

Sweating, his panic increasing, he ran back to Will's locked door and began to thunder with his fists, yelling out his name over and over again. But there was no response of any kind.

Tim listened, trying to calm himself, but all he seemed able to hear was the hammering of his own heart. He took deep breaths and thought of the sea. An image came to him of it being iced over in frozen waves and this seemed, at last, to calm him. What was that? A low moan? A sigh? A grunt? A stifled call?

'I'm coming, Will,' he yelled, and hurled himself at the door. The heavy oak didn't yield and he staggered, rubbing his shoulder. He tried another

half dozen times until he was bruised and breath-
less. Tim forced himself to stop and think, waves
of fear sweeping over him. This was useless; he
had to find a key. But where?

Tim was lucky, for after a brief, frantic search
he discovered the master keys in the wheel-house,
clearly marked. He raced back down the ladder,
along the silent corridor and, with shaking hands
and many faltering attempts, finally managed to
open the door.

Will was lying on the bed, his hands and feet
tied, half propped up, a gag tight across his mouth.
Tim ripped it off, making his stepfather howl with
pain, and as he began to work on Will's wrists, he
shouted, 'Vinci – he's dead. And the others have
gone.'

'He can't be . . .' Will's voice sounded rusty, full
of despair and shock. Tim was convinced that this
time his stepfather wasn't lying. 'Where is he?'

'In the water.'

Will said nothing, looking devastated, staring
ahead unseeingly, whilst Tim finally undid the cord
from his wrists and began to work on his feet,
wrestling with the knots. Where could they be?
Mum, Fran, Dino. And had Will somehow been
Vinci's assassin?

'Luigi jumped me,' said Will. 'He must have
been working for the Don. Carlotti obviously
never meant to let him get away and appointed

Luigi to be his assassin. I'm sorry – very sorry. I thought the Don was being his usual compassionate self, but maybe in the end he couldn't take the risk of Vinci starting up again. I should have realized all that.' He spoke slowly and carefully.

Tim stood back, the knots at last undone, still trying to make sense of what his stepfather was saying.

'There is, of course, another possibility,' Will added, angrily rubbing his lacerated wrists. 'Maybe Luigi is working against the Don too now. He may have done some thinking. If the Don, Francesca and Vinci were assassinated, Luigi could make a take-over bid. He's been on Carlotti's staff the longest – and is certainly the most loyal. To think I almost lost you. If only I'd sussed all this out.'

'But Luigi's only in charge of security,' said Tim in bewilderment, latching on to one tiny point in his stepfather's stream of conjecture.

'He was far more than that. More like a personal assistant.' Will was becoming increasingly frantic. 'He may try and get into the hospital. And now Fran's been taken—'

'You mean, Luigi will kill her?' Tim found the enormity of what his stepfather was saying almost impossible to grasp. 'What about Mum?' he pleaded, close to tears.

'I'm sure your mother and Dino are safe. They've *got* to be.'

Tim stared at him blankly, numbed now by the immensity of it all. 'But where *are* they?'

'I'd guess they'd be in the house on the cliffs above the bay. It's the Don's vacation home and no one was allowed to build anywhere near it. They *have* to be up there.'

Slowly, Tim began to accept what Will was saying, but he felt mentally exhausted, unable to see ahead, to have the slightest idea of what they might do. A sudden thought struck him. 'Why didn't Luigi take you as well?'

'He hates me,' said Will slowly. 'He's always been jealous of my relationship with the Don. He wanted to make me sweat, worry myself to death about them. He probably rounded up the others at gunpoint and then came in here and knocked me unconscious. God knows how you escaped. Perhaps he was interrupted.'

'Who by?'

'The coastguard boat maybe. It's on regular patrol around the coast.'

'When did Luigi start all this?' asked Tim, the suspicions beating in his head as hard as ever. The kaleidoscope had returned, absorbing them both; his thoughts were in swirling confusion – no doubt as they were meant to be.

'Just before dawn,' replied Will.

'What about Tonino? Is he with him?'

'I'm sure he is.'

Tim tried to think logically and failed. 'But if that's what happened, why didn't Luigi come back when the coastguard boat had gone?'

'He probably reckoned they'd be patrolling up and down the coast all day; they're always checking out drug smuggling. Or maybe he didn't think it was worth it. He's got the others, after all.'

Tim didn't reply. The latest ploy in the battle for the Don's empire had left him punch-drunk.

'Do you believe me, Tim?' Will asked quietly. 'I realize I don't have much of a track record for the truth.'

Will's story seemed increasingly implausible to Tim, but he was so confused that he didn't know how to reply.

'Do you want to feel the damn great bump on the back of my head?' his stepfather persisted.

'I don't *need* to.' Tim was flustered now. 'How are we going to get them out of that house?' Instinctively he decided not to challenge Will's explanation. What would be the point, wondered Tim. He was alone with the stranger again – the man whose identity seemed to become more elusive with each twist and turn of the extraordinary events surrounding them – events that had not only moved completely out of control but had ended in death for the first time; that they were also compounded by his stepfather's lies, Tim had not the slightest doubt.

'We'll have to take Luigi by surprise,' said Will, his authority slowly returning.

He thinks I believe him, thought Tim, so I have to go along with it all. But somewhere in the back of his mind there was still a tiny spark of hope that this time Will really was on the level.

'I can't bear to think of your mother in a situation like this – a situation I dropped her into in all my stupidity. And the same applies to Dino and Fran. Luigi and Tonino may have been involved in planning this *coup* against the Don for a long time. They would know how much the local people love him, so it would be essential for Luigi to make them think that Vinci muscled in, got thrashed, and that for a while the Don's staff are going to run a caretaker administration.'

'Until?'

'Until they bring in an old man – even older than Carlotti. Then the caretakers will become more powerful behind their puppet. The king is dead. Long live another king. I'm beginning to see it all now.'

'Who would the new "king" be?'

'I don't know. It might be Baptiste Colombo. He is another cousin – but enfeebled enough to be manipulated by Luigi. Colombo would make an acceptable front and would enjoy the status.'

'Why would so many of his staff be disloyal to the Don?' asked Tim. 'I can understand why Vinci's people would, but—'

'I can't give you all the answers, Tim – I don't know them. Maybe they've just grown greedy. If Luigi can get into that hospital—' Will sounded impatient now, but Tim was persistent. He *had* to find out if Will was lying. But how? Tim was in a maze – and his stepfather kept altering the route.

'You were his debt collector. Why didn't you realize what was going on?'

'I didn't want to – didn't want to see that the whole situation was breaking down. Self-deceit is a powerful force, Tim. Do you know what I mean?'

'Yes – I do know what you mean.'

There was a long silence during which Tim realized his stepfather had either dealt his most cunning card – or was being straight with him. Then Tim decided to try another ploy. Suppose he pretended to believe him. Would Will see through that pretence?

'I'm sorry.'

'What for?' asked Will huskily.

'For doubting you.' Tim couldn't detect distrust in his stepfather's eyes, but then he was up against a professional actor.

'You have every reason.'

'No—'

'You have *every* reason, Tim,' said Will

vehemently. 'But I'll prove myself to you – I promise.'

'Why didn't Luigi kill me and Fran in the cove?' Tim asked suddenly. 'Why did he rescue us instead?'

'It's possible that Luigi changed his mind and suddenly decided he couldn't take a risk like that before he knew the *coup* was successful. That night-time swim of yours was a damn nuisance but I suppose he had no choice but to go along with it. He probably had a walkie-talkie. Maybe Luigi waved them off at the last moment. I'm sure the original intention had been to kill you both.'

'Luigi *was* slow in bringing the jeep round. Fran was angry.'

'Probably making some last minute arrangements.' He paused. 'Look Tim – I've got a throat like a sawmill. Can you go and get me some water – with ice? Then I'll tell you what I think we have to do.'

Whilst he was getting a glass out of the galley cupboard, Tim tried to marshal his thoughts. Everything safe and familiar had suddenly vanished and he felt deeply afraid. He longed for his mother or even Dino, but all he had left was Will, and although he could still feel the strong bond between them – the shared history of sheltering from the threat of reality in reading, fantasizing and running – he knew he would be a fool to trust

159

him. Tim filled the glass and got out the ice, the mundane task soothing him, making him think with greater clarity. There was no choice; he had to go along with him. Tim shivered. It would be like playing a game of chess with a grand master, and the irony was that, despite everything, he was still fond of the grand master. Please, God, prayed Tim. Please, God, let Will for once be telling the truth.

Will grabbed the glass in an unsteady hand and drained it in one long draught. 'I've been thinking that I'm being completely irresponsible. I can't expose you to any more danger. I want you to stay here while I swim over to the mainland. I 'm going to try and get—'

But Tim interrupted him angrily, shocked at the tables being so quickly turned on him. 'Don't think for a minute that you're leaving me behind,' he said furiously.

'I can't run the risk of—'

'I'll follow you.'

'I could lock you in your cabin.'

The unexpected impasse was too much for Tim's pent-up emotions and he picked up the glass and hurled it at his stepfather. Will ducked and it shattered against the wall. Then Tim threw himself at him, pounding and hitting him with his fists, yelling, screaming, fiercely denying that he should be left behind for any reason at all. Will fell back on the bed, trying to protect himself from the blows as Tim landed on top of him, continuing to rain them down. For a few minutes he seemed dazed by the violence of the attack, but then he grabbed Tim's wrists, held him off and rolled him over, crushing his weight down on his legs to stop him kicking.

'You've *got* to stop.'

They were both sweating now, clammy in each other's grip.

'Tim.'

But he still struggled, frantically trying to free himself. He wouldn't allow Will to outmanœuvre him.

'OK, I'll take you.' Will gave in.

Tim subsided at last, breathing in great racking gasps, but the feeling of triumph spread inside him.

'I love her. I love her,' he repeated over and over again.

'You mean your mother?'

'Yes. And Fran too. Who the hell do you think?' But Tim also meant Will and he began to kick and struggle again in his frustrated fury.

'Calm down.' Will's grip on him tightened.

'You'll *take* me?'

'I said I would. Why don't you listen?'

'I've *got* to go.'

'You will. Now, if I let you up – are you going to stop trying to kill me?'

Will released him and Tim sat up, rubbing his eyes. He saw that Will was looking at him with great concern. Then Will turned away, shoulders shaking, his whole body bowed with emotion, and Tim got off the bed and went over to him, grabbing his arm, desperate to know what was wrong.

'What's the matter?'

He continued to sob.

'Have I hurt you?'

Still the relentless, hollow crying.

'Have I hurt you, Will?'

'No.' He turned round, wiping his eyes.

'What's the matter then?'

'I lied to you for so long.'

'That's over.'

'I lied to myself.'

'That's over too.'

'Oh Tim—' Will took him in his arms and held him tightly. 'We'll build up Whispers – all of us. We'll always be together. Always.' He was fierce now in his determination. Slowly, Will fought for control, then he went over to the cupboard and from behind a pile of blankets pulled out an automatic pistol.

The appearance of the weapon was a severe shock, forcibly reminding Tim of the terrible danger this man presented to him – the same man who was so capable of losing his self-control.

'Luigi didn't find this.' Will gave Tim a watery smile.

'Do you think he has reinforcements in that house?' They were back in their game now. The emotion had stopped.

'No. The rest of those bastards will be too busy trying to get at the Don. While you were fetching that water I called the hospital.'

'He's still alive?'

'Yes. I told security what might develop and they're doubling up the guard. If we move fast we can get at Luigi before his back-up arrives, but we'll *have* to move.' He paused. 'We'll both swim over to the mainland and then split up. All I want you to do is walk up the steps to the house.'

'Where will you be?' Tim didn't even think of the consequences of doing what his stepfather told him. He just wanted to outsmart him.

'Coming round the back. Then I'll take Luigi by surprise.'

'There's no other way?'

'No.'

'What about the police?'

'Here? In Sicily—'

'Aren't *any* of them loyal to the Don? There must be *some*.'

'We can't afford to take the risk. Listen to me.'

Will was cool and confident now, once again talking to Tim as if he was an adult. 'When you get to the house you're going to convince Luigi that we've fallen out – and you want to be with your mum. Once you're inside – try and open a window for me.' He paused. 'But don't put yourself in any unnecessary danger. For God's *sake* don't do that.' Fleetingly their eyes met, but Tim was the first to look away. He didn't know how to interpret the intensity of his stepfather's pain.

CHAPTER EIGHTEEN

ONCE THEY were on deck, Tim saw the glint of
binoculars at the window of the house on the cliff
above. 'He's watching us,' he said.

'Not for long. Are you a good swimmer?' Will
seemed to be miraculously calm again.

'I'm OK.'

'If we dive from the other side of the yacht and
aim for those rocks we can get under cover. But
he'll be able to see us in the sea – there's nothing
we can do about that. Just have to trust to luck.
We'll discuss the rest of the plan when we get
ashore.'

'What about the gun?'

'I've got a waterproof bag. I'll strap it on.'

As Will made his final preparations, Tim began
to feel even more apprehensive. Surely he was no
real match for his stepfather's manipulations.

The sea was still a sluggish deep meridian blue,
the waves striking the beach with little slapping

sounds and withdrawing with a gentle sigh. Tim and Will lowered themselves into the water and slowly swam around the *Marie*. Will looked briefly at Vinci's corpse, but Tim couldn't face seeing it again. Then the pair headed for the rocks which ran out like a long, gnarled finger into the sea. Swimming on for another ten minutes in the lazy current, they negotiated the weed-hung reef and started to head for a rocky promontory of scrub and dusty foliage. The time was now well past eleven and the sun was a searing fiery ball, lacerating their shoulders directly as they clambered up on the ledge.

'This is where we split up,' said Will.

'Which way are you going?' asked Tim, trying to be brave.

'Round the back of the headland. It's quite a detour which will probably take me half an hour. All you do is to walk up that little path by the rosemary bushes and keep straight on round the cove. There you'll find a flight of steps. Go up those and knock at the door.' He grinned. 'Ask if they're serving elevenses.'

Tim felt numb. 'They'll have seen us swimming.'

'Probably.' Will seemed almost detached.

'So they'll know you're on your way.'

'You know what to say – tell them we've fallen—'

'They might not believe me.' Then he had an

inspiration. 'But they would if you gave me a black eye.' That would be the ultimate test, Tim thought. Would Will hit him or not? He might not have the faintest idea of what to expect at the door of the house on the cliffs, but at least he would know how much his stepfather cared for him. 'Come on then,' he said. 'Hit me.'

'I can't do that,' replied Will.

'You must – it's a good idea. It will really make them think we've had a row.'

'I don't care *what* they think,' said his stepfather. 'Not if I have to hurt you.'

Tim grinned at him, remembering the companionship they had shared and how little they now trusted each other. It was good that Will wouldn't hit him – at least Tim thought it was. Then another thought came into his mind – a desperate thought that he knew was almost an hysterical reaction. He *had* to show Will how much he cared for him. Maybe if he did that, his stepfather would come clean with him.

'I love you, Will,' said Tim. 'I love you this much.'

He took a run at a small, salt-encrusted tree and ran slap into it with a resounding thud, falling to the stony ground, lying stunned but rejoicing in the knowledge that he had given *himself* the black eye – had done it for Will. The Don's sense of honour was in him.

'For God's sake—' Will ran over to him, looking as stunned as Tim felt. 'What the hell do you think you're doing?' Again his eyes were full of tears.

'Getting myself what we needed. So what's it like?'

Will stared at the crimson welt that would soon turn black and blue. 'How could you *do* that?'

'Because I love you.'

'I'm not worth it.' Will spoke with total conviction, shocked and confused and above all, for once, his real self. Fran had said that his real self lay in a different place. Well – it did, thought Tim. It lay in a place of pain.

'You're everything to me and Mum and Dino,' said Tim. 'And maybe to Fran as well in the future,' he added hopefully.

'She hates me and would never trust me.'

'She will.'

'Yeah.' Will kept staring at the puffy bruise that was coming up under Tim's eye as if he couldn't believe what he was seeing.

'Take care, Tim.'

They shook hands and then Will pulled Tim close, hugging him fiercely.

'Tell them I hit you. Maybe tried to kill you. Try to make it sound as if you hate me – that I'm the villain they all think I am.'

'I know what to do.'

'Keep them talking. Don't let on you've seen

Vinci, and I'll get in there somehow and disarm Luigi.' To Tim's misery, Will was back to his old tricks – he was sure he was. The pain had been for nothing.

'And then?' he asked his stepfather patiently.

'I don't know. If we could make it to France we'd be safe, but we'd have to sail through the night. The main thing is to get Luigi rattled. Ever done any acting?'

'I used to like drama at primary school.'

'So did I.' He grinned disarmingly. 'That's something else we've got in common. Maybe we should join the local amateur dramatics when we get back to Kent.'

No, thought Tim. You should be at the National Theatre.

Tim began to run up the steep little path. He was devastated. But then he began to question his own motives, to wonder if his self-sacrifice had not been just a trick – a trick to match Will's own deception.

CHAPTER NINETEEN

TIM COULD see the *Marie* at anchor below, moving slightly in the current, a gull perched on her railings. Her elegant wooden decks were pristine in their scrubbed cleanliness and varnish, her fresh paint and highly polished brass glowed in the sunlight. Smaller sea birds hovered scavenger-like around her stern and Tim began to sweat with a deadening claustrophobia. It was almost midday and he longed for a breeze, a gale, a storm – anything to alleviate the sultry calm and oppressive feeling of the world closing in on him. Surely the headland was moving nearer, the tide higher, the sky pressing down, the rocks looming. All he could hear was the sound of his own heavy footsteps and the distant chugging of a fishing boat far out to sea. A bird wheeled over his head. Was it a hawk?

Now he was climbing the steps towards the house, taking care not to crush a snail, smelling the sharp brine of the sea. His agitation increased, becoming a raw apprehension that made his heart race and his stomach flutter. Suppose they were all dead. He had hardly considered that possibility. Suppose – Tim tried to clear his mind of the nightmarish thoughts, but they wouldn't go away and his eye stung and throbbed as he walked on. He had to get there fast; he couldn't delay any longer, a prey to these ominous thoughts. Somehow he struggled into a run and immediately felt himself pushing through a stodgy blanket of warm air.

The dark blue door of the house was tightly shut, and although he listened carefully, Tim couldn't hear a single noise from inside. The title of a corny film came into his mind. *The House of the Dead*. Except that it wasn't such a corny title. Not now. He raised his hand to knock, but it was too leaden, the sultry air too heavy to allow him to make contact with the sun-blistered wood. He tried again and again but the atmosphere seemed to become thicker, the sound of the waves like concrete falling upon concrete.

Tim began to gasp for air, his lungs full of plaster; lead lined his stomach, his eyes smarted painfully. He *had* to knock but the weight of the sky seemed to be pinning down his arm, and when he looked at the ocean it was still, lumpy. He saw the landscape contract into a tunnel which rushed towards him. Tim fell, hitting the door with the full force of his body.

*

He felt cool air, someone bending over him, a voice he couldn't make out, but the crushing weight had gone. Tim's vision cleared and he found himself lying on his back, staring up at Dino. In one hand he held an ice-cream which he hurriedly put down on a stone pedestal.

'Thank God,' he breathed. 'Thank God you are here. Your mother – she is in a terrible state about you. But your eye. What happened to your eye?' He looked almost comically amazed and appalled.

'Will hit me,' he whispered but he knew he was reading a script. Did it sound convincing, he wondered desperately. More to the point, would it convince Luigi? Or didn't Luigi need convincing? What exactly *was* the scenario?

'Where is William?' asked Dino.

'I don't know.'

Dino felt Tim's forehead. 'You have fever.'

'Where *is* everybody?'

'Why are you whispering?'

'Are they OK? Is Mum OK?'

'Of course they are. That's why Luigi took us off the yacht.'

'What?' Tim's head was throbbing. Dino wasn't making the slightest sense.

'To get us away.'

'From who?' Tim stared at him as if he was talking in some incomprehensible language.

'He overpowered William and locked him in his cabin.'

'Will? But he—'

'Luigi will explain.'

'I don't get you,' Tim said blankly.

'Luigi will explain.'

'Wait—' Tim's head spun. 'Why did he leave me on the *Marie*?' The conversation sounded like something from *Alice in Wonderland*.

'Luigi. He tell.'

'Where's Mum?'

'In the bedroom. Luigi gave her a sedative. She wild for you. You come in now.'

Dino pulled him gently to his feet and Tim walked slowly inside, his head spinning.

The house was as stylishly furnished as the yacht and had one large room downstairs, hung with pictures, scattered with light furniture opening on to a terrace. In fact, to Tim the place looked like a film set and had an air of total unreality to match his thoughts. Luigi was sitting on a sofa, half turned to the door. For someone who had made a hasty escape he looked not only at ease but wholly in charge.

When Tim came into the room, he got up immediately, his face lit by a delighted, relieved smile. 'I'm so happy you are safe. But I know

173

William loves you and would not harm you. I have worked with your stepfather for many years and I trust him with you and your mother. Also with Dino. But there my trust has to stop.'

'What's going on?' asked Tim, his legs trembling so much that he couldn't stand up any longer. He sat down heavily beside Luigi.

'William is an ambitious man – as Carla found to her cost, however much he loved her. The Don is blind enough to think he became so devious after her death. I'm sorry – but I believe the seeds were in him – had been in him – for many years. Dino knows that and whilst he was hopeful – because he had to be – he could always read your stepfather's real intentions. William is out for himself – and no one else.'

'If Dino has such a bad opinion of Will – why did he come to England with him?' asked Tim, still feeling light-headed, hardly able to reason.

'Because he allowed himself to believe his lies – about new beginnings. He wanted to make one too, you see.'

'I still don't understand why you left me on the yacht and took the others away.' Gradually Tim's logic was returning. God knows, he thought, he had had enough practice in this world of deception. Could he believe anything anyone was saying? The answer definitely must be no.

'I knew you would slow him up.'

174

'I released him,' said Tim.

'If you hadn't, his associates would have returned for him. It was only an exercise in damage limitation. Listen to me, Tim. Your stepfather is a spider spinning his web. As I've said before, I knew he wouldn't harm you and I also knew his dearest wish was to kill me, so I decided to evacuate the yacht before his reinforcements arrived. I assume they are still laying siege to the hospital. And the Don is out of danger, thank God.'

'But Will warned them to increase security.'

'Did he?' Luigi smiled indulgently. 'Once we were here I knew he would come to the house, but he would also have to look after you which would hold him up, give me breathing space, a chance to lead him into a trap. Do you understand?'

Tim stared at him blankly, grateful for the opportunity to play for more time. 'No.'

'But I am surprised to see he hit you.' Luigi looked puzzled, reluctantly acknowledging there was a flaw in his assessment of Will's personality.

'We had an argument – and he lost his temper.' Tim decided to keep to the story for the moment. 'He does sometimes. He hit Dino – before we came out here.'

'Then he has become more violent.'

'Where is my mother?'

'Asleep. She has been so terribly concerned

175

about my decision to leave you with your step-father.'

'That doesn't give you the right to sedate her.'

'This conversation is not productive,' replied Luigi, his voice crisp, authoritative.

'I suppose you've sedated Fran as well.'

'No. She is asleep.'

Tim could feel his anger rising but he held it back; he mustn't lose control. 'Tell me,' he said slowly, conscious of Dino standing behind him now. 'Is there any other reason for giving my mother a sedative?'

'I had to tell her about William. How he plotted with Vinci to kill the Don.' He paused. 'The Don suspected Will but loved him and hoped against hope that his suspicions would prove unfounded. But he had the sense to ask me to act as his under-cover man and I gradually discovered William and Vinci were conspiring together. Even then I had a problem convincing the Don – almost as great a problem as I've had convincing your mother. And I don't think I've succeeded with her yet. He inspires great love, doesn't he – your William?'

Tim stared at him in silence.

'I'm telling you the truth.' Luigi's intelligent, distinguished face had a patient expression. Tim looked at Dino imploringly.

'I'd suspected. But I was fond of him. Wanted

to be with him. Even now it's hard to accept that he was never the man I thought he was.'

'You see what I mean? Will compels people.' Luigi gave him a gentle, understanding smile.

I must go on keeping him talking, thought Tim. I have to find out who's lying. If only it *could* be Luigi. 'You don't have any proof.'

'You'll see.'

'Who killed Vinci?'

'I did.' Luigi casually accepted responsibility.

'Why didn't you kill my stepfather too?'

'Because I have to take him alive – as the cowboy movies say.' He smiled, inviting complicity but finding none. 'The Don insisted, after he was shot by the man in the helicopter. But he will not be merciful now. He will take the Hawk to Corvo. To the women. For they knew all along. They tried to tell the Don, but he wouldn't listen.'

'Listen, Tim,' said Dino. 'This is true. You *must* believe us.'

The door opened and Francesca came in, her dark hair tangled and her eyes puffy with sleep. But when she saw Tim her whole expression became ecstatic. 'Thank God,' she said, and threw her arms round him. 'He hurt you. Why?'

Tim didn't respond. He *had* to believe his stepfather because he meant so much to him. Because he had always wanted to love him. Suddenly his decision was quite clear. Will *had* to be right and he wouldn't let them all gang up on him. Tim would find the window, open it, admit Will to the house and his stepfather would explain as he had never explained before – and he would convince everybody. 'I'm OK,' Tim muttered and Fran backed away, staring at him curiously.

'He's coming here,' she said. 'Isn't he?'

Tim struggled to think of a convincing reply.

'If he is – I'm ready.' Luigi went to the glass table and took out an automatic from the lower shelf.

'You've accepted the situation now? You know Luigi's told you the truth, don't you?' Fran demanded.

'I've tried to explain,' said Luigi, 'but he won't listen.'

'You're as foolish as my father – Will is the most convincing liar I've ever met,' she added sadly.

'You can't tell me he's evil,' said Tim fiercely. 'No one can.' But he knew now that he was a liar too – and was going to hang on to his lies with the same sure, strong grip as Will.

'I won't have to,' Fran replied more quietly. 'He'll do that himself.'

'Anyway – I want to go to the toilet.'

'Very well,' said Luigi calmly. 'But don't go outside the house. The washroom is through that door and down the passage. Don't be long.'

The corridor was marble floored and hung with pictures of impressionist landscapes. Coming from the bright sun outside, the whitewashed walls seemed cold and the lack of light gave the interior a gloomy, almost dank feel. It was so dark that at first Tim thought there *were* no windows and then he saw that he was wrong. At the very end of the passage, near the toilet door, was a square window which was just big enough to admit his stepfather.

He ran swiftly towards it and pulled at the heavy catch. After a struggle, the window opened and the heady, radiant light poured in. He was still standing beside it when he heard Fran's voice behind him.

'What are you doing?'

'Nothing.'

'You opened that for William, didn't you?'

'No.'

'It wasn't open before.'

'It was.' The argument was getting childish.

'Shut it!'

'Why should I?'

'Then I will.' Fran began to walk towards him, her face flushed, angry, determined.

'You won't.'

'You'll stop me?'

'If I have to.'

'Boys don't fight girls.'

'This one might.' He sounded triumphant in a

juvenile sort of way. Suddenly he hated her. Will trusted him and she wasn't going to keep him out.

'Shut the window.' She was centimetres from him now, her whole body radiating anger.

'No way.'

She was just about to spring at him when to his utter disbelief, Tim heard his stepfather's voice.

When they both ran back into the lounge they saw Will standing there, quite relaxed, the gun in his hand. 'Your security's terrible.' He turned to Tim and smiled. 'You didn't have to help me after all.'

The silence was finally broken by Fran. 'You tried to kill my father. You're no more than an animal.'

Will ignored her, pointing his gun at Luigi's stomach. 'The garage lets into the storeroom – and that lets into the kitchen. I'm surprised you didn't remember.'

'I did,' replied Luigi. 'In fact I made sure that it was open myself. I wanted your stepson and your wife to see you as you really are.'

Will laughed casually. 'You know you mean a lot to me, Tim,' he said, 'but I have to tell you the truth. The real truth – not just the way we'd both like it to be.'

Tim stared at him, something scratching at the door of his mind. It wanted to come in, but he wouldn't let it although he knew the black dog was there, knew that he couldn't keep it at bay any longer. His stepfather's final betrayal had completely exposed Tim's pathetic attempts at self-deception. He had wanted to believe – but now he knew that would no longer be possible.

Marian walked slowly into the room. 'What's going on?' she asked. Then she saw Tim at the same time as she saw Will and his gun. 'Thank God you're safe,' she said. 'They've been telling me lies.'

'They're not lies,' replied Tim. 'Are they, Will?'

It was as if there had been a long pause in time and they were all suspended in limbo – Mum by the door, her hand plucking at the loose flesh around her throat, Dino watching Luigi who had his hand in his pocket, Fran gripping the top of a chair – and Will smiling. He looked relieved. This was Fran's distant place after all.

It was Fran who broke the spell. She went up and slapped Will round the face as hard as she could. He barely reacted and she did it again. Still no one moved.

Tim watched. The truth was like Torridge. It was also about loss – a loss as great as death.

'My father trusted you,' Fran said. 'He loved you – like Tim and Marian and Dino. But not me.'

Will still had his gun levelled at Luigi's stomach. His hand didn't shake at all. Then he pulled the trigger again and again, but there was only a series of useless little clicks. A trickle of sweat ran down his forehead.

'I took the bullets out on the yacht,' said Luigi quietly.

'When was that?' Will sounded only casually interested.

'While you were in the wheel-house.'

'I see.' He put the gun down on a little coffee table.

'You must come with me now.' Luigi drew his own weapon out of a drawer and levelled it at Will.

'Where're we going?' he asked as if someone had proposed a walk.

'Outside,' said Luigi sharply.

'Don't hurt him,' said Marian. 'Please don't hurt him.' She moved a step forward, staggered slightly and then regained her balance. Her lips were moving but no sound came out.

No one else spoke and Will's eyes rested on Tim's. Then he looked away.

'You come,' said Luigi impatiently.

Will turned and walked towards the open door with Luigi following, his gun only a few centimetres away from his back.

Tim went over to his mother and held her in his arms. Then he gently released her and, before anyone could stop him, ran through the open door.

Will and Luigi were standing on the top of the

cliffs overlooking the sea. Had it not been for the gun they could have been having a casual conversation on a hot day in the cool shadow of a little vine-covered summer house.

'Dad,' yelled Tim as he ran towards them. 'Wait for me, Dad.'

'I'm waiting,' Will said. But he didn't wait long enough; for Will turned his back on both of them and without the slightest hesitation dived over the cliff.

Luigi barred Tim's path, the gun still in his hand. 'Don't come any nearer.'

'I don't care if you shoot me.' Tim pushed past him and stood on the edge, looking down at the slight heat-haze that was clouding the sea.

'He's dead,' said Luigi. 'I promise you – he's dead. No one could survive a dive from this height.'

But Tim was certain Will was swimming somewhere in the glassy sea and was sure he would see him again. *Read to me, Tim*, said his stepfather's voice in his mind. A bird wheeled above him – a bird he had seen before and had imagined was a hawk. But it wasn't – it was a gull flying high in the thermals.

Tim walked slowly back to the house with Luigi following him at a respectful distance. The final moment of truth had come and he was glad. Will couldn't lie to him any more and there was only one certainty left: they loved each other. That, at least, had always been true and could never be twisted.